TEMPTED BY HER
GREEK TYCOON

KATRINA CUDMORE

MILLS & BOON

First published in Great Britain 2017
by Mills & Boon, an imprint of HarperCollins*Publishers*
1 London Bridge Street, London, SE1 9GF

Large Print edition 2018

© 2017 Katrina Cudmore

ISBN: 978-0-263-07373-7

MIX
Paper from
responsible sources
FSC® C007454

This book is produced from independently certified
FSC™ paper to ensure responsible forest management.
For more information visit www.harpercollins.co.uk/green.

Printed and bound in Great Britain
by CPI Group (UK) Ltd, Croydon, CR0 4YY

For Ross,
in this year that you start a new adventure.

May life be full of happiness and love.

Mum

TEMPTED BY HER
GREEK TYCOON

CHAPTER ONE

THE LOCAL FISHERMEN were unloading the day's catch from their *caïques* when Loukas Christou motored his boat into the old harbour of Talos Town. Once moored, he'd nodded distractedly to the calls of, '*Kalispera*, Loukas!' from the restaurant and boutique owners whose businesses lined the sun-soaked seafront promenade before hurrying up the narrow whitewashed laneway that was a pedestrian shortcut to the entrance gates of The Korinna Hotel.

Earlier that day, while away on business he had called his brother Nikos on their home island of Talos for an update on The Korinna renovations, expecting to be told of yet another hiccup. Instead Nikos had announced—with a large dollop of unwarranted self-congratulation—that the renovations were officially complete and the hotel was ready to reopen.

Nikos had gone on to assure Loukas that he wasn't joking and then had shouted down the phone that he wasn't exaggerating and that as Head of Project Management for the Christou Group he should 'damn well know'.

Loukas had growled back that it was about time. And not for the first time had pointed out to Nikos that the reopening of The Korinna was a fortnight behind schedule.

It was at that point that Nikos had hung up on him. No surprise there.

At least The Korinna would open in time for Pascha—the Easter celebrations. Their guests were to arrive on Megali Pempti—Holy Thursday—and would be a mixture of loyal customers and specially invited travel journalists and bloggers. All would have sky-high expectations of their stay at the five-star hotel.

With less than a week to test all the facilities, and iron out the inevitable issues that would crop up following the extensive renovations, Loukas had decided to cut short his trip to some of the other hotels in the group to come home to Talos early.

Beyond the laneway, in the shade of the resort's avenue that led to the hotel which was carved through a pine forest, he yanked off his tie and opened his shirt collar. The successful reopening of The Korinna was about more than just his ambitious plan to renovate all their existing hotels and acquire other iconic premises throughout Europe to add to their stable of five-star hotels. It was also about the Christou siblings working in co-operation for once…and mending the fractures that Loukas, both in his role as head of the family and CEO of the group, had failed to heal since their parents had died eight years ago.

It was a co-operation that would be vital if they were going to survive in the demanding luxury hotel market. To date, that reconciliation hadn't exactly been going to plan—as witnessed by his call with Nikos earlier.

Towards the end of the avenue he paused and glanced down to his left. Beyond the hotel's candyfloss orchard of flowering orange, lemon and peach trees was the family villa. A rocky outcrop separated the villa from the rest of Talos Town. Originally a sea captain's mansion, it had sat on twenty acres of land when first built. But Loukas's father had seen its potential and, after purchasing the villa, had built The Korinna on the land.

He really should go down to the villa and drop off his weekend bag, have a shower, and something to eat. But, keen to see the completed hotel, he rushed on down a sharp incline in the avenue until the pine forest gave way to the vista of The Korinna itself.

A new two-storey extension had been constructed on one side of the hotel—a reception area on the ground floor, the headquarters for the Christou Group on the first. The sea-facing hotel restaurant and the bars at the front of the original building had uninterrupted views of the Saronic Gulf, as had the seven levels of bedrooms above them.

For a brief moment, taking in just how well the architects had married the old hotel with not only the new reception but also the new spa that stood on the crest of the hill above the hotel, he felt the constant heavy weight in his chest lift. Maybe the endless building problems, the significant hit to his profit line, the tense calls with his banks, the disruption of his business and the arguments with Nikos and his other siblings would be worth it.

But that moment proved to be *very* brief. Nano-second-brief, in fact.

He narrowed his eyes and moved closer to the reception area. The sliding entrance doors didn't budge. No wonder, as they were firmly locked shut.

And that, no doubt, was because the floor beyond them was only half tiled, the walls still unpainted and none of the bespoke Italian furniture was in place.

He sucked in some air.

Nikos had obviously been banking on him not returning to the island until the weekend, as he had originally planned, so he would not to have to admit that once again they had missed their deadline.

He was going to throttle Nikos. No. In fact he was going to banish him to a monastery on some remote island where he'd have no access to women or drink.

He peered through the reception area doors again.

Was he even more stressed than he'd thought he was? Was he losing his mind?

He would have sworn he'd just seen a pirate saunter through the lounge area beyond Reception, waving a cutlass in the air.

Sudden ear-splitting music startled him and he whacked his head on the reception door's glass pane.

Ready to murder someone, he twisted around, holding a hand to his throbbing forehead, and instantly knew where to find his party-loving brother.

But then, having taken no more than two steps in the direction of the music, he had come to a complete stop.

In the name of all the saints!

Hurtling down the steep incline of the avenue on a bicycle, her long blonde hair flowing behind her like a jet stream, wearing nothing but a silver bikini top and a scrap of blue material that revealed every tantalising inch of her long golden legs, a woman appeared to be about to crash into the door. Into a glass pane that had cost a fortune and had added to the renovation delays by being delivered weeks behind schedule.

Inches from the precious window, she came to a screeching halt. Then, without a care, she hopped off and placed her bicycle in the bike rack to one side of the doors. With an air of ease and happiness she unravelled the scrap of material from around her hips, the deceptively long length of fine blue silk gauze catching in the light sea breeze and floating out behind her like the train of a sea goddess. Beneath she was wearing nothing but silver bikini bottoms.

He should look away. Be a gentleman. But his

eyes remained glued to the way her hips twirled seductively as she began to wrap the material around her narrow waist and then down over her beautifully curved hips. She continued smoothing the material over her thighs, and didn't stop until she had bound her ankles together. Thus wrapped, from the waist down, she straightened up and adjusted the material whilst staring at her reflection in the window and giving an excited smile.

Why was she dressed as a mermaid?

Again, what on earth was going on? This was a five-star resort, not some theme park.

Only able to take tiny steps, the mermaid inched her way towards where he was still concealed by a canopy pillar. He was about to step forward and make her aware that he was there, but before he could do so she turned, her mouth dropping open when she spied him.

Then, in the quickest recovery he'd ever seen, she gave him a smile and a wave, her eyes shining with delight. 'Oh, hi! I'm so glad you were able to make it back in time for the party. Did Nikos call you?'

Baffled by her question, he asked, 'What party? Why would Nikos call me?'

Her dark brows pulled together. 'Nikos had to

leave unexpectedly this afternoon, but he had organised a staff party for this evening, to celebrate the reopening of the hotel… He asked me to host it in his absence.'

He pointed behind him to the unfinished reception area, his index finger stabbing the air, his frustration with Nikos and his frustration over the fact that despite his best efforts he could never manage to control any of his siblings leaking out in growled response.

'A party? The hotel isn't even finished. Now is *not* the time for a party!'

The mermaid's smile dimmed. 'He thought that the staff deserved a thank-you.' She pointed vaguely in the direction of the terrace. 'I'd better go and check that everything's going okay. I'm running late and by the sounds of it the party has already started.'

He stepped closer to her, trying to keep his eyes from drifting down to her softly curved body. Her smile wavered even more as his eyes duelled with hers.

He yanked his gaze away. Cracked his jaw. And then he asked bluntly, 'Who are you?'

She hesitated for a moment, as though confused

by his question, and then with a laugh stepped towards him.

'Oh, I'm sorry. I've seen so many photos of you and heard so much about you from your siblings that I forgot we have never met.' She held out her hand to him. 'I'm Georgie Jones. Your new PA.'

Given Loukas's dismayed expression, it took a Herculean effort for Georgie to keep her smile in place. Heartbroken or not, Nikos Christou was going to get a piece of her mind when he got back to Talos.

'My *what*?'

She dropped her hand at his aghast tone.

Crikey, Loukas was very different from his brothers. Even more so than the family photos suggested. Sombre, intense, dark... And he was enormous—at least six foot four. With the build to match.

Light golden-brown eyes, a classically handsome face, thick dark brown hair... The only flaw in his perfection was the seriously hacked off tension emanating from his every pore—that and the murderous glint in his eye.

Her move to Talos wasn't supposed to be ending up like this, with her broke and at the mercy of a Greek god who looked as if he had reached the end of his patience.

Moving to Talos had been her dad's dream. After living in endless countries with her restless father, Georgie had been sceptical about his declaration that this was where he wanted to settle. Last summer, when she had finally agreed to visit this small island off the coast of Athens in the Argo-Saronic Gulf with him, she had been sure that this would be yet another failed quest by him to find happiness.

But from the moment she'd seen Talos she had understood why he had fallen in love with this island of emerald waters, golden beaches and dense pine forests. Fallen in love with the whitewashed, blue-shuttered, terracotta-roofed houses that tumbled down the island's craggy coastline. Fallen in love with its tranquillity, with the way time slowed down here.

And as her dad had drawn up his plans to renovate the run-down farmhouse he'd been in the process of buying she had seen first-hand how the island had transformed him. The light, the heat, the stunning sea view from the farmhouse...

The friendliness of their new neighbours and the slow pace of the island had eased her dad's perpetual nervous energy. At the end of their week-long visit, she too had believed that he had finally found a place he could be happy in.

But her poor dad had never got to fulfil his dream. A fatal ruptured aortic aneurysm a month after he had bought the property had ended it all.

Georgie needed to fulfil his dream for him. It was going to be her last goodbye to her soft-hearted dad, who had never got over her mum walking out on them. She intended to keep the house, run it as a guest house. She would run a sea-swimming business during the summer months and leave the island during the winter months for work elsewhere.

Three months ago—just four weeks after her dad had died—she had left her job in Spain and moved here, convinced that her savings would enable her to renovate the property and establish her business.

But unforeseen building delays had eaten up the emergency fund she had factored into her budget and she was rapidly running out of money. The building work was coming to an end, and she had the funds to pay for that, but not for the final payment on the furniture she had ordered for the guest rooms.

She needed to work for a few weeks to earn enough for the final instalment, otherwise she would be forced to cancel her summer bookings and move elsewhere to rebuild her funds.

She flexed her hands, feeling her broken nails from weeks of endless gardening and DIY pinching the callused skin of her palms, and faced her new boss. Well, she *hoped* he was her new boss.

Keep smiling, Georgie. You need this job. There's no other work on the island at the moment.

'Didn't Nikos tell you? He recruited me while you were away. It's only a temporary role, to tide you over until a permanent replacement can be found.'

She gave him a friendly smile, keen to build bridges with her new boss and neighbour, but that only made his scowl deepen further.

For a brief second his gaze moved down over her body. And then he looked away, as though irritated with himself. He shuffled the beaten-up-looking soft tan leather weekend case he was carrying into his opposite hand.

'Where are my other siblings?'

'Marios had a scuba-diving appointment and

Angeliki has gone to Athens. I think she has a date tonight.'

His long fingers rubbed against his temple, as though he were defeated by her answer. She gave him another small smile, wishing she could think of something to say that would help. That would ease the lines of tension pulling at the corners of his eyes.

'Nikos owes you an apology. He had no authority to recruit you. Let's talk in my office.'

Though her heart plummeted to the floor at Loukas's job-terminating-sounding tone, she had to think of the party, and the staff members who had been so excited for days about the celebration.

'I'm supposed to be hosting the party. Can we talk tomorrow?' She paused and then, unable to stop herself, she added, 'Nikos's costume is in his office. You could wear it for the party... It's a Captain Hook costume. I think it would suit you.'

He looked at her incredulously, and then his eyes narrowed as he realised that she was teasing him. His scowl told her that, unlike Nikos, he wasn't one for playful banter. He really *was* different...unfortunately.

'I've work to do. I need to wrap this party up. There's too much that still has to be completed before we open. I will speak to the staff and then we will talk in my office,' he said, before heading in the direction of the hotel terrace along a path lined with thickly blossoming lavender.

She chased after him but her mermaid tail slowed her progress. Unable to catch him, she shouted out in desperation. 'Loukas! *No!*'

He turned around and stared at her, clearly peeved. Under his unimpressed gaze she waddled towards him, feeling less like an elegant mermaid and more like a hung-over duck.

'The party has only just started. The staff will be so disappointed. They've put huge effort into designing their costumes.'

His gaze travelled down over her costume and then he looked back up with a raised eyebrow. As if to ask, *And precisely why should I be worried about any of this*?

But then his gaze moved back down over her body again, this time lingering at her breasts, at her waist. His eyes darkened.

Pinpricks of awareness flooded her body. This was her boss. Her neighbour. Her friends' brother. She had no business being so aware of him physically.

She stepped back, overwhelmed by his size, by the heat licking her insides.

At her movement, the dark appreciation in his eyes turned to annoyance. His mouth twisted unhappily.

For long seconds he studied her coolly. 'I won't stop the party but you and I still need to talk.'

And then, much to her consternation he held out his arm.

'Let me help you.' Those brown eyes stared at her intently. 'You seem to be floundering out of your natural habitat.'

He was messing with her...wasn't he?

His expression remained stern as he waited for her to respond. She wanted to say no, that she'd manage, but to do so would somehow feel as if she was giving in to him. That she would be admitting to feeling like a mermaid out of water around him.

She flashed her best sassy smile at him, clasped her hand with intent on his tanned forearm, and gritted her teeth as the nerve-endings on her fingers tingled at the warmth of his skin, the strength of his flexed forearm.

'Mermaids belong in the sea, Miss Jones. I hope you manage to survive the evening.'

Her eyes shot over to study him. He *had* to be joking this time… Maybe he was as capable of teasing as his siblings were, but yet again his expression gave nothing away.

At an excruciatingly slow pace and in silence they made their way around the corner to the hotel's sun terrace.

The terrace—so elegant with its borders of lush shrubs interspersed with olive and citrus trees, the bright pinks and purples of bougainvillea and pelargonium trained along the external walls, and its plush outdoor seating areas—was crowded with all the hotel staff, dressed for the nautical themed party.

They separated and she detoured to speak to The Korinna's head chef, Jean-Louis, who was dressed as Poseidon, complete with curly wig, beard and golden trident.

As she laughed with Jean-Louis over their respective costumes, and then checked with him that all was okay with the catering for the event, she found herself tracing Loukas's progress through the crowd as pirates, sharks and surf babes eagerly stopped him to chat. It was clear that he was respected and liked by his staff. Why was his relationship with his three siblings so different, then? All three had variously grumbled about him in the past, describing him as everything from a control freak to a nightmare with zero sense of fun.

Loukas was the consummate host, giving his complete if rather serious attention to those he spoke to. But as she was dragged into having her photograph taken with some of the hotel's personal trainers Georgie sensed a growing tension, a greater unease in him as he made his way towards the terrace steps where the party DJ was stationed.

Once there, he spoke to the DJ, who immediately ended the song blasting out of the speakers. He waited until the crowd grew silent before he started to speak.

'The Korinna reopens its doors next week. Thank you for all your hard work and co-operation so far in completing the renovations. We now need to give one final push over the coming days to complete the work so we can deliver the five-star service we always promise our valued guests.'

He moved out to the edge of the steps to get closer to the crowd. His deep voice—which was in keeping with his hulking size and delivered little punches to her stomach every time he spoke—dropped to an even lower grave timbre.

'As you already know, we have specially invited influencers, journalists and bloggers coming for the first time, but we also have some of our regular clients and their entire families staying with us over the Pascha weekend. We need to balance the needs of both groups, and our focus has to be on guest satisfaction at all times. No request is too big, and I want each of you to be proactive and anticipate the guests' needs. At no other time has the Christou business motto been more apt: *We deliver perfection.*'

His shoulders stiffened and his gaze slowly ran across the crowd.

'The future of The Korinna is reliant on us excelling in everything we do from the moment we open our doors again. And everyone else on Talos needs us to succeed too—we need to lead the way in making Talos a year-round destination, especially during the winter months when so many businesses on the island struggle.'

Loukas stepped back and for a moment stared down at the pale sandstone of the patio. When he looked back up there was a vulnerability in the way his mouth worked, the way he blinked hard.

'The past few years have been difficult for us all, but it's now time for The Korinna to shine again.' He paused, his voice catching. 'As many of you know, it was my father's dream that in addition to our hotels here in Greece we would also own some of Europe's leading five-star hotels. Soon I hope to announce the acquisition of some of those premises. But for now let's make The Korinna dazzle—make it the gold standard for what we in the Christou Group promise to deliver to our guests, both current and future. Let's do my parents proud.'

Around her people shuffled and cleared their throats. She rapidly blinked her eyes, sideswiped by Loukas's emotion. This was the man who had looked as if he wanted to commit murder less than fifteen minutes ago.

She remembered Angeliki's poorly disguised attempt at bravado when she had described losing both her parents at only ten years of age. The same bravado Georgie had used to adopt herself when having to explain her mum's absence as a child.

Loukas's gaze swept across the crowd and settled on her. Her heart dipped and soared at his grave expression.

'None of us can allow anything to get in the way of The Korinna's success.'

Loukas entered his office and threw his weekend bag on the office sofa.

He rolled his neck against the steel rod that seemed to have inserted itself down the centre of his spine.

Why had he felt so damn emotional during his speech to the staff?

He sat down at his desk and scrubbed his face with a hand. Inhaling a weary breath, he fired up his computer. Flicking through his emails, he clicked on one from his legal team. He read it and sighed.

His instinct had been right—there really was no way out of the clause that had been inserted into the lease by the religious order who had sold the Convento San Francesco over a hundred years ago.

The convent, in the heart of Florence, had since become an exclusive five-star boutique hotel—a hotel his father had coveted since he and Loukas's mother had visited on their honeymoon and just about been able to afford a drink in the bar. They had both fallen in love with its walled garden and cloisters, and his father—perhaps foolishly—had pledged to his mother that one day he would buy it in memory of their wedding and their honeymoon.

Loukas wanted it. For his parents. This was the first time that it had come up for sale in over a century. He might never get this opportunity again. He *had* to buy this hotel for his father. He couldn't fail him yet again.

There was only one problem—to buy it, he had to be married. The religious order, for reasons that had been lost in time, had specified that the convent could only be sold to a married person.

His legal team had spent the past month attempting to have the clause removed. But it was watertight. As he had expected. In anticipation of this outcome he had employed a dating agency who specialised in executive clients.

He was not interested in finding love. He'd never had any intention of getting married. He had spent his childhood constantly fighting for his parents' love—his father's in particular—and constantly being rejected when he had not lived up to his expectations. He had learnt that loving others made him vulnerable and open to the constant fear and pain of rejection. Love was an exhausting emotional rollercoaster he had no interest in or intention of riding.

What he needed was a wife in name only, and in the past few weeks he had come to realise that he could turn this need for a wife of convenience into an opportunity to recruit extra talent into the business—someone who would help drive the business forward but would also have the toughness to tackle the ongoing problems with his family: namely Nikos's irresponsibility, Marios's stubbornness and Angeliki's lack of independence.

It was a point that had been driven home when he'd recently returned from a business trip abroad to his apartment in Athens to find Angeliki drunk and almost incoherent... She'd been coherent enough though to tell him that she hated her two-timing boyfriend, Dimitris, but that she couldn't break it off because he had the best body she'd ever seen. And all kinds of other stuff no brother should ever hear from his baby sister.

Angeliki needed a strong female role model—for far too long she had been indulged by her older brothers. She needed someone who would push her to want to achieve more in life than the approval of some lowlife guy.

The dating agency had put forward some promising candidates—successful and ambitious women. He had even dated some. But so far they had all come up short.

Tonight's email from his legal team confirming that there was no way out of the clause, together with all the other debacles—an unfinished hotel, VIP guests set to arrive in less than a week, his siblings nowhere to be seen—had brought home the fact that he needed a wife with greater than ever urgency.

He picked up his office phone and called his dating agency account manager, Zeta.

'Loukas... Hi...' Zeta sounded more and more nervous every time he called.

'I have called the three profiles you sent through today. The first had nothing to offer the business.' Zeta tried to interrupt him but he continued on, 'The second candidate laughed when I explained that Talos was a two-hour journey by land and sea from Athens...'

He swung around in his chair to face his office window and stared out towards the Saronic Gulf as he continued.

'And the third couldn't answer me when I asked her how she would deal with the scenario of an eighteen-year-old girl calling at four in the morning from a payphone in Athens asking if she knew where her phone and purse was.'

Zeta let out a weary sigh at the other end of the phone. 'We're running out of suitable candidates.'

'Spread your net wider. I need a wife within the next month. A wife who will accept the nature of our marriage—that it will be in effect a business contract for a two-year period, with generous terms and conditions. The Christou Group is about to expand rapidly. We have already acquired five new hotels in the past year and plan on many more. This will be an ideal time for an ambitious person to be at the centre of that growth. I need someone who is driven, astute, already successful in her career, willing to live on Talos and support me in managing my family. That isn't a lot to ask, is it?'

Zeta started to make some strangled-sounding noises at the end of the line. In no mood to hear her usual argument that he needed to be more flexible, he ended the call—but not before telling Zeta that he would quadruple her fee if she found him a suitable wife within the next month.

'Is now a good time to talk?'

He twisted around to find the mermaid standing at his door, waiting for his answer.

Thrown by the sight of her hand, distractedly playing with the thin silver strap of her bikini top, and seeing the other resting on the smooth taut skin of her midriff, he looked away, silently cursing Nikos. *Again.*

Georgie Jones—all blonde hair, shiny eyes and sunshine personality—was exactly Nikos's type. He didn't need to go to Detective School to figure out that she was either Nikos's newest love interest or soon would be. No wonder Nikos had given her the position as PA. How convenient to have her so nearby.

The idea of moving Nikos away to a monastery on a faraway island was rapidly becoming the best plan he'd had in a long time. But first he had to deal with returning this mermaid to wherever she belonged.

'Please come in.'

She shuffled into the office, her full and rather enticing lips, painted a coral-pink, pulling into an open smile that slowly faded as she stopped in front of his desk.

She squared her shoulders and her hazel eyes held his steadily. 'It would be a huge honour to work for you, and in a hotel as prestigious as The

Korinna. I won't lie or beat around the bush—I need this job.'

She gave him a quick smile that at first seemed open, but on closer inspection he saw that her eyes held a steely determination.

'However, I respect the fact that you weren't aware of my appointment and that it has put us both in a difficult position. I think I have a potential compromise, if you agree. And that is that I initially work for you for a trial period of a few days.'

Time slowed down to excruciatingly long seconds as Loukas studied her with obvious exasperation. Would he accept her proposal?

Life had taught her to be diplomatic, to negotiate and gently persuade rather than fight her way to acceptance by others. After years of being a newcomer she knew only too well that she had to give people space in order to come to realise that she posed no threat. And that included her new boss.

His office faced out towards the azure beauty of the Saronic Gulf, but when he stood up his huge Greek warrior size seemed to devour all the evening light that had been pouring in through the folding glass doors that led to a private balcony.

He moved to rest against a bookcase and asked, 'Exactly what experience have you of being a PA?'

'I've worked as a PA in an architectural firm in Spain for the past eighteen months. Before that I was a theatre hand, a trainee pastry chef, a dog-walker...' She paused, seeing that Loukas wasn't overly impressed, and quickly added, 'I'm flexible and I use my initiative, and I also speak Portuguese, Spanish, Italian...and passable Greek.'

His eyes narrowed in suspicion, he approached her as though he didn't buy a word about her linguistic skills. 'You speak all those languages?'

While her brain objected to his cynical tone, her heart was conducting a most peculiar dance in her chest. Goosebumps were popping up on her skin as her eyes were drawn to the smooth skin of his chest visible beneath the open neck of his shirt. She blinked as heat blasted inside her stomach.

She dragged her eyes away from the dark toffee skin tone and then, intending to let them travel up to meet his eyes, found herself waylaid by his mouth—*was his lower lip slightly fuller than the upper one?*—and then his nose, its straightness and perfection suiting his serious personality.

Eventually she managed to answer, 'I moved around a lot as a child because of my dad's work.'

'Why are you here on Talos?'

Light golden-brown eyes marred by tension lines at the corners held hers. She needed to get Loukas to relax in her company.

She stepped back and gave her best excited smile. 'I'm renovating a property.'

The tension lines tightened even more. 'The old Alavanos property?'

His question came out in a rumble, his voice even lower than usual.

The nod of her head elicited a deep sigh of disbelief from him.

'So, let me get this right… Nikos has employed as my PA someone who is soon going to be a business rival of ours?'

If only. The Talos Escape Guesthouse, as she had decided to call it, wouldn't be opening anytime soon if she didn't pull together enough money to actually furnish the guest rooms. But she wasn't going to admit that to anyone. Sunny side up. That was her motto.

'I'm going to open up a small guesthouse in the summer months, catering for the swimming holiday business. It's hardly going to be a rival to The Korinna.'

Loukas shifted away from her and went and

stood behind his desk. 'Miss Jones, you can't work here. I apologise that Nikos had you believing otherwise.'

He sat down at his desk, briefly gestured to the door and began to riffle through the paperwork on his desk.

Georgie opted not to take up his invitation to leave. She couldn't let go of this financial lifeline.

Engrossed in his paperwork, he was either oblivious to her presence or choosing to ignore her, so she said to the rather beautiful wavy dark brown hair on the top of his head, 'Why?'

He lifted that noble head of his slowly and eyed her unhappily. Throwing the pen in his hand to the desk, he said impatiently, 'Thanks to Nikos, my PA Eleni ran away last week. I have now made it company policy that there is to be no relationships between employees. A policy that is to be implemented at all twenty-six hotels within the Christou Group. I can hardly go against that policy within days of its implementation.'

'I'm not following... How does that impact me in my role as your PA?'

He crossed his arms and threw her a sceptical stare.

Confused, she said, 'I would *never* date my

boss… And anyway, I… I overheard your telephone conversation just now. Aren't you looking for a wife? I'm not wife material.'

His eyebrows shot up. 'I was talking about you and *Nikos*.'

'Oh.' Despite the inferno igniting her cheeks she heard herself laugh. 'Nikos and me! Are you *serious*? He's like a little brother. We're friends—nothing more. Just as I'm friends with Marios and Angeliki.'

'You're friends with them too?'

'I've got to know them over the past few months through Nikos. Marios and I share an interest in sea-swimming and Angeliki is teaching me Greek—she's stayed over with me some nights.'

'Really?'

Why did he sound so appalled…so surprised?

She rested a hand on the flimsy material of her mermaid tail, itching to whip it off, to go and put on some proper clothes. But perhaps she should fess up to everything in order to clear the air completely between them. Although she got the feeling he wasn't going to like it.

'There's something else we need to talk about, as I'm presuming that you aren't aware of it… I've moved into your family villa.'

* * *

She had what?

The mermaid wove a finger through the ends of her golden hair and gave him an uncertain smile before adding, 'Nikos said I should stay at the villa as I will need to work late most days and the four-mile cycle back to my house in the dark is pretty terrifying, with all those open drops down to the sea.'

Had Nikos lost his mind? Yes, those who lived in the furthest reaches of the island often had to endure less than favourable road conditions on this car-less island. But he was the only person who still lived in the family villa.

Earlier this year, when he had made it clear how unhappy he was with their work, one by one the others had moved out. Nikos and Angeliki had originally shared an apartment overlooking the harbour in town, but had reluctantly agreed to move in to the new management apartment adjacent to The Korinna, that Loukas had commissioned as part of the renovations.

Nikos needed to be on hand when Loukas— who, along with his role as CEO of the Christou Group was also general manager of The Korinna—

was away on business. Marios lived on his boat, moored at the town's old harbour.

Was having Georgie move in to the villa another of Nikos's ways of getting him back for pushing him so hard? Or was Georgie lying to him? Were she and Nikos an item and this was their way of living close to one another whilst pretending that they weren't breaking the company's newest human resources policy?

'Why didn't Nikos have you move in with him and Angeliki?'

She gave him a quizzical look. 'I don't think Nikos is in the mood for company at the moment…he's pretty heartbroken.'

Nikos? Heartbroken? When had that happened? Why the hell didn't he know anything about it?

'Because of Eleni?'

Georgie considered him for a moment, as though wondering why he should even have to ask that question. 'Yes, of *course* because of Eleni.'

His guilt and frustration at his fractured relationship with his siblings coiled in his stomach. He didn't need this stranger reminding him of how much he was messing up in his role as head of the family.

But she obviously wasn't a stranger to his siblings…and she knew more about their lives than he did. That fact stuck in his gut like a piece of indigestible news.

'How did you meet Nikos?'

'Through Eleni. She and I met one day on the beach. We became friends and she and Nikos used to visit me.'

They had? 'I thought their relationship was a short affair.'

'They've been together since the start of this year.' For a moment she looked at him and worried at her lip with her teeth. Then, in a rush, she added, 'I guess you weren't aware as you travel so much with work. That's why Nikos left today—he's followed Eleni to Thessaloníki to try to speak to her.'

Had it come to this? A stranger having to find excuses for him as to why he had no idea what was going on in his brother's life?

Along with his reconnaissance visits to some of the most exclusive hotels in Europe, he had deliberately spent most of the winter and the spring on week-long stays in their different hotels dotted throughout Greece—principally to carry out organisational and management reviews and to get direct customer feedback from their guests.

But he had also hoped that his siblings would become more responsible and resourceful in his absence.

The steel rod in his spine tightened. 'It's not appropriate that a member of staff lives in my villa. Nikos should never have told you that you could move in.'

'I know it's not ideal, but all the staff accommodation is full. I promise that I won't get in your way, and it will only be until the rush of the reopening is over.'

Why was she so keen to stay? 'The reopening isn't for another week—why have you moved in now?'

Her bright expression faded. 'My builder removed my old windows last week, believing that the new ones were to arrive that day, but they didn't. Now I've no windows. I didn't really mind, but the guesthouse is single-storey and one morning I woke to find a herd of goats staring at me in bed. It was pretty terrifying. I couldn't sleep after that.'

Thrown by the laughter that danced at the back of his throat at a vision of Georgie Jones awaking to a herd of the local inquisitive goats, Loukas picked up the bronze paperweight he had inherited from his father. His fingers traced the raised profile of a turtle while he tried to clear his head of that image and consider what he should do.

He would need a PA—especially in the coming week. But the last thing he needed was an employee who might be a distraction for Nikos. He should get rid of Georgie. But to do so would only give his siblings more ammunition for them to rally against him and complain about his lack of heart. Anyway, he couldn't bring himself to pack her off home to a house with no windows. His lips twitched as he pictured her waking to see the staring goats.

'Like I said, I couldn't help but overhear about your need for a wife… I might be able to help you.'

His head snapped up. 'Are you offering?'

Her mouth dropped open. It was hard not to be offended by the horror in her eyes.

'Heavens, no—I'm not the marrying kind, and anyway I heard your requirements. I'm not sure I fulfil any of them.'

She tilted her head and he saw a glimpse of astute calculation in her eyes before she gave him a bright smile.

'But I do have an extensive network of friends

throughout Europe as well as here on Talos… Suitable women who might be interested in meeting with you. Employ me and you not only get a PA but also your own in-house matchmaker.'

This mermaid was full of surprises. Intrigued, he asked, 'Have you any actual experience in matching people?'

'I've set up a lot of successful blind dates in the past… And last summer I attended the wedding of a colleague from Malaga and my car mechanic, who I got together.'

Was he so desperate that he was seriously considering employing a woman dressed as a mermaid to be his PA and matchmaker? In a word: *yes*. The current owners were giving him a month to complete his purchase of the convent. After that they would sell to the next bidder.

Never slow to make a decision, he said, 'Okay, here's the deal: I'll employ you until I can recruit a replacement PA. If by some miracle you manage to find me a woman who will happily live here on Talos, who understands that our marriage will be one of convenience, is successful in her career and prepared to play a senior role in the Christou Group, and who is tough, especially when dealing with people, then I'll pay you two months' wages as a bonus.'

He gestured to the paperwork on his desk.

'I have work to do. I'll see you here tomorrow morning at seven.'

She made a face. 'What about love?'

'It's not part of the equation.'

By the puzzlement in her expression he could see that he needed to explain further.

'I'm marrying for two reasons, Ms Jones. To fulfil a clause that is present in the lease of an Italian hotel I wish to purchase, and to have someone who will assist me in the day-to-day operation of the business, with a specific focus on people management and supporting me in managing my family.'

Georgie eyed him dubiously for a moment. 'Am I right in assuming that a marriage contract would be drawn up?'

'My legal director is working on it at the moment. It will be a two-year contract with a generous salary and bonus package.'

She shrugged. 'It's not conventional…but who knows? It might work for the right woman. Someone who would like the opportunity to be part of the Christou Group.'

She moved forward and shook his hand firmly.

'I'm looking forward to working here,' she said. Then she turned to leave and slowly, oh, so slowly, took tiny steps towards the door.

He tried to go back to his paperwork. But his eyes refused to obey.

She flicked her head and for a moment he caught a glimpse of the knot holding her bikini top beneath the heavy weight of her long hair. His fingers itched with the impulse to pull at that string. To undress this mermaid.

At the door she wobbled as she turned to him. And then, with that oh, so sweet and cheery smile, warm hazel eyes twinkling, she said, 'See you bright and early.'

When she had disappeared from view he stood and stared out towards the Saronic Gulf.

He needed to focus on what mattered. Successfully relaunching The Korinna. Getting his family functioning again. Finding himself a wife.

Why, then, did he get the feeling he was going to struggle to ignore his new PA?

CHAPTER TWO

LOUKAS THREW OFF his bedclothes, his heart pumping.

What was that noise?

In the pitch-dark he fumbled for his phone.

Four forty-one.

There it was again. A soft banging.

He eased out of the bed and grabbed the gym shorts he had left out the night before.

He slowly opened his bedroom door.

The sound was coming from downstairs.

He bunched his fists and crept along the corridor, his bare feet moving silently across the tiled floor.

His nostrils twitched.

He inhaled deeply and closed his eyes, bewildered for a moment, his mind a dizzying blend of childhood memories, his heart kicking against his chest.

He shook his head, trying to make sense of it all, trying to shake off the disorientation of waking from a deep sleep to the reminder of his mother's baking.

Slowly the penny dropped.

His house guest.

Thee mou! He was going to kill Nikos…and probably her too.

Downstairs, he followed the corridor to the kitchen-dining room at the far end of the villa.

The dining area was in darkness, but the recessed kitchen lights reflected like satellites at night off the angled bank of patio doors out onto the terrace.

He followed the sweet, seductive scent of baking, heard the soft thud of an oven door closing, cursing Nikos every step of the way.

He had back-to-back meetings later today. There were management problems at their hotel on Hydra, and yet more planning problems with their hotel on Santorini. He needed his sleep disturbed like he needed a hole in the head.

He pulled up short of the kitchen.

Who the hell…?

Thrown, he stared at the woman who was busy transferring items from a baking tray to a wire cooling rack. Barefoot, and dressed in lilac pyjama shorts and a cropped white T-shirt, she was humming to herself.

Who was *she?*

And then she turned ever so slightly, and those full lips, high cheekbones and glittering eyes were unmistakable.

'Georgie?'

Georgie screamed and dropped the baking tray. The tray ricocheted off the edge of the kitchen counter with a clang, flipped onto its side and plummeted straight down, the corner catching the middle of her foot.

She yelped at the sharp pain and jumped back, hopping on her uninjured foot. But then she stood on one of the just-out-of-the-oven croissants scattered on the floor. The croissant crunched under her weight before becoming firmly attached to her sole. She yelped again and shot up to sit on the kitchen counter, frantically shaking her foot in a bid to remove the scorching hot pastry.

The pastry dropped to the floor with a disgruntled plop.

She stared down at her throbbing feet in disbelief before daring to turn towards Loukas.

'Georgie?' he said again.

Why did he sound so confused?

And then she remembered. She lifted her hand and ran her fingers over her shoulder-length light ash-brown hair. 'I was wearing a wig last night.'

His gaze immediately moved to her feet, and as he moved towards her, her already hysterical heart switched into frenzied mode when it sank in that he was wearing nothing other than a pair of black gym shorts.

Her eyes skimmed over him briefly before she stared again at her throbbing feet, her mind flashing with images of what she had just witnessed. Broad shoulders, muscle tightly wrapped against bone... A powerful muscular chest... Taut stomach... Long athletic legs... Hard thighs... Sharply defined calves.

He was beautiful. It made her itch—no mere mortal deserved such perfection. No wonder he didn't have to try too hard with his social skills. People would bow down at his flawless feet regardless.

She watched in disbelief as he crouched before her, his huge frame curling effortlessly and fluidly to balance on one knee. His thumb moved against her foot, gently testing the area where there was an angry-looking cut, and a bruise starting to blossom around it. Then he tenderly lifted her other foot to examine its sole.

Unable to breathe, she dug her fingers into the countertop, fighting against the tide of emotions welling in her. Loukas was the first person to touch her in what felt like a lifetime. She wanted to pull away, overwhelmed. And yet she wanted this moment to last for ever.

Her foot still cradled in his hand, he looked up and grimaced, his expression worried. 'I'll get the first aid kit.'

'There's no need...' Her words trailed away as he disappeared into the utility room.

He was back within seconds.

Quickly and efficiently, he applied a burn spray to her sole and swabbed a disinfectant wipe across the broken skin of the other foot. She gasped as it stung.

He paused and gazed up at her. 'Are you okay?'

She nodded, her voice stolen by her surprise at the gentleness of his tone, the tenderness of his touch.

'The cut isn't deep, but I'm worried that you might have broken something.'

She wriggled her toes. 'It's fine—honestly. The

pain is already practically gone. I got a shock, that's all. I thought you were asleep.'

Balancing her foot on top of his bended knee, he reached into the first aid kit and took out a sticking plaster.

'Why were you baking in the middle of the night?'

With delicate care he placed the plaster on her foot, his thumbs softly running over each end, gently applying pressure to ensure it was firmly in place.

'I couldn't sleep. I take pastries into work most days… Marios especially loves my croissants. I prepared some dough yesterday, before work, and decided to bake the croissants now as it helps me to relax.' She inhaled a deep breath and gave a guilty grimace. 'I'm guessing that I woke you?'

He didn't answer her question, but instead said, 'I'll be back in a few minutes…don't move.'

Georgie threw her head back and stared at the kitchen ceiling when he left the room. She was mortified at being so clumsy. And thrown by Loukas's patience and care.

What a great start to her employment. All night she had tossed and turned, her mind reeling with thoughts. Her escalating bills. The endless chasing of her builder. The fact that her new boss, who for some reason made her feel as if she was plugged into the electricity mains, was less than happy to employ her. The fact that she had volunteered to be a matchmaker to said boss in order to retain her job.

Was she out of her mind? Undoubtedly a neat queue would form if she advertised the fact that Loukas Christou was looking for a wife—who *wouldn't* want to marry a hotel tycoon with dark movie-star looks and the body of a professional athlete? But what would happen when the women learnt it was a practical business marriage, love not included?

Would that work for some women? Perhaps. Look at how successful arranged marriages where in some cultures. But where was she going to find such a woman within the next few weeks? She had needed a distraction. She'd tried reading and then counting sheep, but they had disturbingly morphed into belligerent goats. After that she had known that her usual fail-safe of baking was the only answer.

Why was the prospect of getting Loukas onside so daunting? After all, she had done this a hundred times before. For as long as she could remember in every new country, new city, new school, new job, she had had no option but to smile her way into acceptance. Despite the fear of being rejected, which had been alive and mocking in the pit of her stomach every time she'd approached a wary new face.

And even when she had become accepted by those new schoolmates, and later work colleagues, despite her exuberant front and her deep, sincere desire to connect with people, she had never truly managed to. After her mum had left, and then all the friends she'd lost time and time again when her dad had uprooted them, she had realised that it was easier to keep people at arm's length. To be a social butterfly. To keep those friendships on the surface. For their sakes and hers.

That was until she'd met Alain. At first, as the owner and head chef of the restaurant where she'd begun her training to be a pastry chef, he had been her boss. She had fallen in love with his enthusiasm and passion and they had quickly become a couple.

But she had hurt him terribly when she'd left him. Feeling as if she were unable to breathe. Panicked at how serious their relationship had become. Questioning everything about their relationship and convincing herself that she was only with him because he made her feel safe. That she wouldn't feel so freaked out if she'd met 'Mr Right'.

A few relationships later it had slowly dawned on her that maybe 'Mr Right' didn't exist for her... Not through any fault of the men she'd met. No, the problem lay squarely at her door—she'd been moving about for so long her need for change was bone-deep, her restlessness, her love for travel and exploring new places—all were too strong within her for any relationship to survive.

Loukas was wearing a grey hooded sweatshirt when he returned to the kitchen. In silence he approached her and then, again crouching before her, he began to place a pair of snow-white sports socks on her feet.

'These will be too big, but they are padded and will be more comfortable when you walk.' Standing, he asked, 'Do you want to give it a try?'

She nodded, but before she could react further his hands were on her waist. Gently he eased her forward on the counter, and her hands reflexively reached out to hold his upper arms before he lifted her slowly down onto the marble floor of the kitchen. Her hands refused to drop away from his arms—in fact her fingers insisting on remaining wrapped around the powerful strength of his biceps.

Drop your hands, Georgie. What are you doing?

But his hands aren't dropping from my waist either, and it's so nice here, being held, inches away from him, inhaling his scent...citrus, but with a hint of basil and cedar.

He's your boss—you're his matchmaker, for crying out loud. Let go!

But instead of letting go she dared to look up into his eyes.

He looked as perplexed as she was feeling.

She gave him a wobbly smile. 'Hi.'

He jerked his head back, as though suddenly waking up to his surroundings.

In unison they moved apart.

Her heart a churning mess, her legs wobbly, she took a few tentative steps. It stung, but seeing his concerned expression at her measured movements she upped her pace and gave him a bright smile.

'I think I'll live.'

'Good.' He gestured to the stools by the breakfast counter. 'Go and sit down. I'll clean up.'

He refused to allow her to help, so Georgie sat at the counter feeling sheepish. But as he cleared away the baking equipment, wiped the counter surfaces and swept the floor, the silence between them and the darkness outside, the fact that they were all alone in his villa, had an intoxicating feeling of intimacy.

When he'd finished tidying up he turned and considered her.

She smiled and said, 'Thank you.'

He nodded, and for the longest time they stared at one another, something shifting between them.

He's your boss, Georgie. Stop it!

She yanked her gaze away and for want of something to do reached across the kitchen island and pulled the cooling rack towards her.

She had managed to place seven croissants on the rack before she'd dropped the baking tray on her foot. She held out a croissant to him, wanting to thank him but also to reach out to him for reasons she didn't fully understand.

He eyed the croissant dubiously, so she explained. 'A peace offering—to apologise for waking you.'

He reached for the croissant with a hint of a smile and broke it into two. 'It'd better be good to make up for having me believe I had a burglar.'

She held her breath as he took a bite. He nodded his head and took another bite.

He raised the remaining small piece of pastry in his hand. 'You're safe…this is really good.'

She tried to hide just how pleased she was that he liked her baking and said, 'I worked for a while as a trainee pastry chef in a restaurant in Lyon.'

He took a bite from the other half. 'Why did you stop when you're obviously so talented?'

She shrugged and said, 'I wanted to move on to something else…to a new city.'

He folded his arms and considered her for a moment. 'Like dog-walking?'

Annoyed by his judgemental tone, she answered instantly. 'I was a dog-walker when I was eighteen. After Lyon I moved to Lisbon and worked in a theatre there as a stagehand.' Unable to stop a defensive edge entering her voice, she added, 'I hate being confined. I like change.'

He popped the last remaining piece of croissant in his mouth and chewed, eyes narrowed as he considered her words. Eventually he said, 'Having no responsibilities?'

The croissants she had baked were plump and a dark golden colour. She eyed them for a few seconds before darting her gaze back to him. This time she did not bother with a smile. 'You sound critical.'

He looked at her in silence for the longest while before saying, 'We've a long day ahead of us. We'd better go and get some sleep.'

She stood, her feet stinging a little. She bit back a grimace. Not wanting them to part with the tension that was between them right now, she said, 'I really am sorry that I woke you. And thanks for looking after me tonight, for allowing me to stay. You have a wonderful home...the tall ceilings, the décor, the courtyard garden...it's all so beautiful.'

His expression relaxed and his gaze moved from her to the kitchen and dining area beyond. 'My father and mother loved this house but they didn't have time to invest in it. It was comfortable, but pretty ramshackle when I was growing up—nobody had seriously invested in it for over a hundred years. I renovated it a few years back.'

She swallowed and tried to find the right words, knowing just how painful it was to lose a parent. 'Angeliki told me about your parents dying. I'm sorry...it must have been a difficult time.'

His gaze briefly met hers, and there it was again, that *something* between them—a connection, a recognition despite the tension between them. Was it the silence of the house, the darkness outside, that was causing them to talk like this?

'We got through it.' He looked away and said with the hint of a sigh, 'My siblings didn't want the villa renovated. Maybe they were right.'

The tension lines around his eyes were back in force, as though he was burdened by that admission.

Puzzled, she asked, 'Why do you think that?'

'I thought that if I renovated the villa Marios and Nikos would realise that life had changed...that we all needed to move on and that they needed to start living differently and assume more responsibility. For Angeliki I wanted to create new memories. But they resented it that I'd changed so much about the family home. There were a lot of arguments over it.'

She went and stood next to him, where he was standing by the dishwasher. He clearly blamed himself for the arguments.

'It sounds like you were doing it for the right reasons...because you care for them.'

He shook his head. 'They don't see it that way. Anyway, it's time we called it a night. Can I help you upstairs?'

Had she gone too far? Why was she risking her job by talking on such a personal level with her boss? Would he regret everything that had passed between them tonight?

'I'll manage by myself.' She gave him a smile. 'I think my tap-dancing career is still in the bag.' Her smile faded at his bewildered look. 'I'll... I'll just get myself a glass of water. See you tomorrow.'

At the door, he turned and watched her for a long moment, as though unhappy to leave her there by herself. She deliberately strode to the glasses cupboard, forcing herself not to wince.

She grabbed a glass and waved it towards him. Reassuring him that all was well.

Eventually he said, 'Come into the office whenever you're ready in the morning.'

She appreciated the gesture, but there was no way she was going to give him any excuse to find fault with her performance. 'I'll be there at seven. I'm looking forward to it.'

The following morning the rising sun daubed thick smears of burnt orange fading to red on the sky as Loukas left for work. Across the harbour the island's lighthouse beam flickered and dimmed in the growing daylight.

He had been born and raised on Talos. Had

stood at his father's side as a six-year-old when he had laid the first foundation stone for The Korinna. Had listened to his father's plans and ambitions to open a hotel on Talos that would become world-renowned for its beauty and hospitality. A hotel that would bring employment and prosperity to the island. The first of many planned hotels.

His father had dug a trench in the hard and resisting earth of Talos, sweat on his brow, his back bent as his shovel sent shock waves through the parched soil, and his words had been the passionate dream of a man who had come from nothing.

'Loukas, we must work hard, you and me. We need to look after the family. We are Christous, and we will never fail.'

His father's dream had come true. For almost two decades he had never ceased working, never taken even a single day off. He had pushed himself relentlessly. And pushed his family just as hard.

Within ten years the Christou Group hotel chain had had twelve other properties in the Argo-Saronic Gulf and five years later twenty-one hotels spread throughout Greece, with plans in place to purchase more in Italy and Croatia.

But then Loukas's mother had been diagnosed

with terminal cancer. And for once his father hadn't been able to change the future by sheer will and determination alone. It had broken him. And two months after the diagnosis he had died from a heart attack.

Loukas closed his eyes for a moment, remembering his mother's shouts for help. Remembering how he had run to his father's office and found him unconscious on the floor. He hadn't known what to do. Blind panic had immobilised him for crucial seconds. He remembered his feeble attempts to perform CPR, his screams at Nikos to call the emergency services, Nikos pressing the wrong numbers...having to try again.

He had failed his father that day. He should have saved him. He had failed his brothers and his sister. Because a year later when his mother had died they'd been left parentless.

At the age of twenty-three he had inherited not only the majority ownership of the family business but also responsibility for all three of his underage siblings.

From the moment his father had died in his arms he had sworn that he would do everything in his power never to fail him again, that his focus would only be on protecting the business and the family.

And now, eight years on, the business had survived the worst recession in Greek history. But the family had grown more and more fractured as the years had passed, and Loukas knew he was failing as the family's head.

The family and the business were firmly interlocked. Each needed to function well for the other to survive. His siblings all owned a percentage share in the business, and were able to veto any of his decisions—which they did on occasion. Not on the basis of any business rationale but just to remind him of their power, that they had a voice.

The garden's cobbled mosaic pathway came to an end at the pale blue garden door, where the track running through the orchard took its place. This was where, when they weren't working in the hotel he had hung out with his siblings as children. Their parents would try to send them home for a siesta, but instead the four of them would climb the trees, and when the fruit was ripe sit in the shade, sometimes drowsily falling asleep, sugar-drunk on the sweet juices of the peaches.

But now that closeness had disappeared, and the most frustrating thing about this broken family was that he could see that all three of his siblings were brimming with potential. They just refused to co-operate with him and remained too relaxed in their roles. Why couldn't they assume their responsibilities without fighting him on everything? Why couldn't they worry like he did? Even break a sweat on occasion?

And now he had this new PA Georgie Jones to contend with too. Last night, being with her in the kitchen, had been bewildering. Taking care of her, touching her, had felt so right. When in truth it had been all wrong.

He inhaled a deep breath. He was overthinking this. Georgie was a temporary PA. The next week would pass in a whirl of work and deadlines and then she would be gone. Georgie Jones was inconsequential. Opening The Korinna and finding himself a wife. Those were his priorities.

He grimaced at the idea of marrying. But he had no choice. His father might no longer be here to fulfil the promise to his mother to buy the Convento San Francesco, but *he* was and he would do everything in his power to acquire it.

'Loukas—wait up!'

He turned to Georgie's call. She waved to him and jogged up the hill towards him with small measured steps. In the daylight she was even more beautiful without the wig, her natural hair colour more in keeping with her lightly tanned skin, the smattering of freckles on her cheeks and her hazel eyes.

She came to a stop beside him and smiled. 'Morning.' Then, with an embarrassed grimace, she added, 'I hope you managed to get back to sleep.'

He wanted to say, *Well, what do you think? When all I could picture when I closed my eyes were your long legs in those ridiculously cute shorts, the lift of your breasts beneath your top... With the memory of your vanilla scent when I knelt before you, lifted you down from the counter. The narrowness of your waist. How tempted I was to pull you closer—*

Instead he pointed to the white trainers she was wearing beneath slim-fitting black trousers. 'How are your feet?'

'Fine. But I thought it would be more sensible to wear something comfortable walking along this path.' She lifted her hands to reveal a towering pair of black stilettos dangling from her fingers. 'I'll wear these in the office.'

He swallowed hard. 'There's no need. Allow your feet to heal.'

Liar! You just don't want the temptation of watching her wear those shoes.

Her dusky pink blouse, tucked into the waist-band of her trousers moved as the breeze caught it. The silk pushed against her skin, outlining her lace bra beneath.

He looked away. His jaw locked tight. 'Let's go. I'll brief you on what I need you to do today before my conference call at seven-thirty.'

They walked together along the path, with the voice in his head mocking him all the way.

Oh, yeah—she's inconsequential, all right.

That evening, exhausted and dazed, Georgie sent out her final emails of the day. She had worked non-stop for thirteen hours, coordinating Loukas's next board meeting, planning his promotional trip to Asia and getting updates from the US PR company who, earlier in the week, had launched a direct-to-consumer and social media campaign to publicise the reopening of The Korinna.

Her stomach rolled angrily, demanding some food. After a quick swim in the sea she would cook some dinner.

Her gaze moved to Loukas's open door. He had spent most of the day on teleconferences. She had taken coffee in to him a number of times through-out the day, each time attempting to make small talk, but he had clearly not been interested in engaging with her.

His mood had first gone downhill when she had heard him argue with Marios over the planning of a ceremony that was to be held in their Athenian hotel soon, and then nosedived even further when Nikos had arrived back from Thessaloníki.

She had given Nikos a piece of her mind for not having informed Loukas of her appointment, but her annoyance had faded when she'd realised just how down he was over his meeting with Eleni.

He had just started to explain to her what had happened when Loukas had arrived back from a meeting with the builders in an irritable mood. He had dragged Nikos into his office, and even with the door closed she had heard them arguing about her appointment.

She had sat there, with that old knot of shame that had been her constant companion as a child forming with such a punch in her stomach that it had felt as if it had never gone away.

It was a knot of shame that had appeared soon after her mum had walked out on her—out of their family home in England—when she was seven years old. A knot of shame that had told her there had to be something wrong with her for her mum to have walked away from her so easily; not to have wanted to take her with her. A knot that was a constant reminder that if her mum could walk out on her, then so could anyone else. She wasn't wanted…she wasn't good enough.

She knew her only focus should be on delivering a professional service to Loukas. But he was also her neighbour. She wanted to be able to get along with him. To be accepted by him. And part of her longed to see the Loukas of last night again. The Loukas who had been caring and kind.

Hauling in a steadying breath, she stood and approached his door.

His concentration was fixed on his computer screen, his right hand click-click-clicking away on the mouse, and Loukas did not notice her presence until she cleared her throat.

'I'm finished for the evening.' Unease fluttered in her stomach at his terse nod but she kept on smiling. 'I was going to cook some pasta for dinner—would you like me to make you some too?'

Loukas glanced at his computer screen and then stood. Pulling on his grey suit jacket over his pale blue shirt, he met her gaze. 'Thanks, but I'm meeting someone for dinner.'

She backed out, towards her office. 'Oh. A date? Well, I hope it goes well. It's a lovely evening for it.'

Oh, God, she knew she was blabbering, but the idea of Loukas on a date left her all jittery. She turned and fled before her mouth really got carried away.

Out in her office, after giving herself a quick mental telling-off for not behaving professionally, she swung round to wish him a goodnight, her heart leaping into her throat at finding him standing directly behind her, fixing the collar of his jacket, his movements releasing the scent of his aftershave from the material.

Feeling a little punch-drunk by his sheer size, the chemistry oozing from his hard body, she stared blindly at the spot where part of his jacket collar still remained tucked inside against his shirt. Evening shadow darkened his throat, giving extra emphasis to the wide strength of his neck.

She pointed vaguely. 'Your collar... Your collar...'

He stared at her quizzically.

And then, stupidly, she reached forward and

fixed the collar, her fingers skimming against the warmth of his skin, the hard muscle beneath.

His hand reached up and grasped hers.

Her heart slammed to a stop.

His hand was smooth, warm, embracing.

He looked at her quizzically. But there was also a darkness, an awareness in his gaze.

Heat seeped through her body. 'I… I was… I was just fixing your collar.'

His eyes held hers and she willed herself to look away. But there was something there—a familiarity and yet a newness, a union she didn't understand. His eyes softened and his thumb moved over the inside of her wrist. Just once. But it was enough to send a deep shiver throughout her body, to make her legs suddenly weak.

She gave an uncertain smile.

His eyes narrowed before he dropped her hand and stepped away.

'Have you found any suitable dates for me?'

'I'm working on it.' She paused at his frown and added, 'But most of my friends are looking for love in a relationship—'

He interrupted her before she could continue. 'Which is out of the question.'

She tried to give him a professional smile, but for some reason it died on her lips. 'So you said.'

For a moment he looked down at the off-white smoothness of the painted and polished concrete floor that ran throughout the new offices. He rolled his shoulders in one quick movement and then looked up, his expression businesslike.

'Before you leave can you call the event management company who are organising the movie awards ceremony in our Plaka hotel in Athens? Ask for an update—in particular if any issues have arisen since I spoke to them this afternoon.'

Thrown by the coolness in his eyes, the impatience in his tone, she hesitated before responding. She knew she shouldn't say anything—that it would be easier to nod her agreement and have him walk out through the door—but she knew how much it dented Marios's confidence when Loukas questioned everything he did.

'Shouldn't Marios be doing that?'

His mouth thinned. 'Marios has gone on another scuba-diving trip with a customer of his. Until he starts taking his responsibilities seriously I have no choice but to check with the event company directly to ensure all is okay.'

He moved towards her office door.

The voice of logic in her head was screaming at her to let it go, to think of her bills, telling her that none of this was her business. But her heart was cheering her on to defend Marios.

'But he might feel undermined. I'm sure he'll have checked in with the event company.'

He turned at her words, his angry glare warning her off.

She had hated hearing them arguing this morning. She couldn't stand by and see the tension between the brothers escalate.

'How about I arrange it so that Marios sends you a daily summary, highlighting any issues he believes you need to be aware of?'

His expression darkened. She held her breath, convinced she was about to get the mother of all tongue-lashings.

He opened his mouth. Closed it again. His hand reached up and for a moment stroked his neck. The exact spot where she had touched him.

His eyes narrowed and he considered her for another beat. 'Tell him I want the summary by ten tonight. No later.'

He twisted away and walked down through the now empty open-plan office, his laced black leather Oxford shoes tapping on the concrete floor, his shoulders beneath his suit jacket rigid.

She slumped down onto her chair. Was she wrong to interfere? What did she, an only child, know about the dynamics between siblings? What did she know of the pressures Loukas was under as head of the Christou Group? And shouldn't she be focused on keeping her job, not winding up her boss?

She was about to phone Marios when she heard the clip of Loukas's footsteps on the concrete floor again.

Awareness of him bubbled through her as he came to a stop by her desk, his size, his scent, his energy sending the elements in the air careening off in a different charge.

'I realise that you're trying to help, Georgie, and your suggestion for a report from Marios is good. But I know what I am doing. Please don't interfere.'

She gulped at his serious tone, at the way those golden-brown eyes, firm but not unkind, stayed on hers. Her insides melted. 'I want to help.'

His gaze softened ever so slightly. 'Don't... There's no need.'

She nodded. And then, unable to stop herself, she asked, 'Are you going anywhere nice tonight?'

His gaze narrowed. 'Sakis—on the harbour.'

She tried to look enthusiastic. 'It's beautiful there…really romantic—out on the terrace, especially.' She checked her watch. 'You'll just be in time for the sunset.'

Was that a hint of smile on his lips? 'I'm sure my finance director will be pleased—he loves a good sunset.' And then a genuine softness entered his eyes. 'After you've called Marios go home. You've had a long day.' He shifted on his feet, his eyes trailing away, and cleared his throat. 'Sleep well, Georgie.'

He walked away, and she followed his progress through the office until he disappeared through the double doors.

Her heart spinning with a lightness that could become very addictive.

CHAPTER THREE

LATE THE FOLLOWING AFTERNOON, after a protracted meeting with the landscapers, Loukas rushed along the service corridor that ran from the hotel's conference centre to the headquarters building, keen to get back to his desk. The acquisitions team were waiting for his response on a proposal they had sent through on an opportunity to acquire a historic hotel on the Amalfi coast.

But then he came to a sudden stop. And backed up three steps to the staff noticeboard.

His gaze honed in on the offending item he had seen from the corner of his eye as he had rushed past: a photo of Georgie in her mermaid costume, surrounded by the hotel's male personal trainers who were dressed in nothing but red shorts and carrying way too much testosterone in their gym-honed bodies.

He stared at the photo. Georgie's arm was around the waist of one of the men, her hip angled towards the photographer, the high curve of her bottom in profile.

He gritted his teeth and walked away. But five seconds later he was back at the display case. It wasn't appropriate to have a photo of his PA, half-naked like that, on display for everyone to see. He tried to pull the glass panels at the front of the display case apart, but infuriatingly they were held together by a single silver lock at the base.

He ignored the curious look the head of Housekeeping sent in his direction as she passed by and stabbed out Nikos's number on his phone.

He took the stairs up to the headquarters building, and hung up when the call rang through to Nikos's voicemail.

Why did he never answer his phone?

Within ten seconds he had his answer.

Inside the double doors of the headquarters building, he caught sight of Nikos in Georgie's office, popping open a champagne bottle. Georgie's laughter rolled down through the open-plan office, causing curious staff members to pop their heads up over their partitions.

In an instant he was striding towards his office, and the staff members were dropping down into their cubicles as though taking cover.

He didn't want Nikos flirting with his PA.

In fact, come to think about it, he wasn't too pleased with the way Georgie somehow managed to emotionally and physically ambush him whenever they were together... He remembered how good it had felt last night, when she'd fixed his collar. He should be focused on the business, on reviewing the dating profiles Zeta had sent through. Not constantly distracted by the low humming of his PA, how the scent of her perfume drifted into his office.

At the doorway he came to a stop and cast a critical gaze over the cosy scene. Nikos was propped on the side of the desk, pouring champagne into the glass Georgie was holding, whilst she giggled as the drink foamed and trickled down over the sides of the glass. Eyes dancing in amusement, she lifted her hand and one by one sucked the champagne off her fingertips.

Something low and carnal exploded inside him.

'Alcohol is not allowed in the workplace.'

Nikos twisted around at his words and gave him an amused grin.

Loukas's blood pressure upped a notch. Did Nikos *really* think that there was time for him to flirt with his new PA? With the hotel still not ready to reopen? He had tried to speak to Nikos about Eleni when he had returned from Thessaloníki yesterday, but his brother had refused to talk about it. Was he exaggerating his upset to Georgie to gain her sympathy...maybe a lot more?

He walked closer to the desk. 'And let me remind you that relationships aren't allowed between staff either.'

Nikos gave an incredulous laugh and Georgie gave him a curious look, before handing her glass to Nikos and gesturing towards his office. 'Chef Jean-Louis is here for the menu tasting for the opening celebration lunch on Easter Sunday. He's waiting for you in your office... He wanted my opinion on this champagne before you decide on which one to serve.'

Loukas gave a terse nod, trying to ignore the way Georgie was studying him closely.

Nikos stood and considered him with an amused raise of an eyebrow, and his gaze never broke from Loukas's as he leant over towards Georgie and in a loud stage whisper said, 'I don't think your boss is happy with us. I'll save some for you...meet me for dinner later.'

Over his dead body.

'Georgie needs to work late. I want her to accompany me on a tour of the hotel tonight. We need a fresh pair of eyes to spot if anything is missing or needs to be changed.'

Georgie looked as surprised as he was himself by his announcement. He clamped his teeth together, determined to pretend that he had conceived the idea of a tour long before now. He gritted his teeth even harder when he remembered the acquisition report that he was supposed to be working on. He really didn't have time to act as tour guide... Well, he'd keep it short.

Nikos held the champagne glass up to the light, his expression one of bored amusement. 'It's Friday evening, I think Georgie deserves some time off.'

Loukas levelled a stare at his brother. 'And our guests are arriving next Thursday—to an as yet unfinished hotel.'

Nikos took a long, slow slug of champagne, shrugged and said, 'We'll be ready.' He shifted around towards Georgie. 'So, Georgie, which would you prefer—dinner with me or a hotel inspection with your boss?'

Georgie's gaze swivelled between him and Nikos before settling on Nikos. Of *course* she'd choose Nikos. They were friends. Were they even more?

Loukas clenched his hands, feeling a bolt of jealous disappointment sideswipe him.

But then her gaze moved to him. And remained there.

'I would love to have a tour of the hotel.' Standing, she added, 'And dinner would also be lovely, I know Angeliki is free tonight, and I'll call Marios. Why don't all five of us have dinner together? I was just about to leave and visit some of the businesses down on the harbour, to brief them on the reopening, so I'll book a table while I'm there.'

Nikos knocked back the rest of the champagne in his glass and Loukas studied him, waiting for him to object, to find a reason for them all not to have dinner together. The way he and Marios normally did when he had suggested they meet. And that would suit Loukas just fine.

But, to his surprise, Nikos picked up the champagne bottle, muttered, 'Sounds like a plan to me,' and sauntered into Loukas's office to join Chef Jean-Louis.

Should *he* be the one to say no to dinner? It was likely to be an acrimonious affair, if past family gatherings were anything to go by. Did he really want Georgie witnessing first-hand the tension in his family?

Georgie picked up a file from her desk and slung a wide cream leather handbag over her shoulder before moving towards him. 'I'll be back by seven for the tour. I'll book a table for nine.'

'Dinner isn't a good idea.'

She stepped closer to him. 'There's nothing going on between Nikos and me,' she said in a low whisper, her gaze challenging, daring him to disbelieve her.

She held his stare and he was dragged into the depths of those hazel eyes, his heart pumping faster and faster at the sight of the power, the solemnity, pride and dignity he found there.

He stepped back. 'I know. But we are only days away from opening The Korinna. We should be focused on that.'

She gave a satisfied nod, rearranged the strap of her bag on her shoulder, said, 'Precisely the reason you all need some downtime,' and walked out of the office.

'When I was a stagehand in Lisbon we had a famous elderly actor performing at the theatre, but because he couldn't remember his lines I had to relay them to him via an earpiece. He was a complete sweetheart, and it was all going well—until one night I spilt coffee all over myself, and he shouted out in the middle of an Ibsen death scene, *"Sweet divine, I've ruined my dress".'*

Loukas heard his siblings' laughter fill the outdoor courtyard of the Thea Garden restaurant and Georgie shook her head in a self-deprecating manner, mischief twinkling in her hazel eyes.

She took a sip of the Moschofilero wine he had ordered for the table before moving her gaze to meet his briefly.

Angeliki, who was sitting next to Georgie, pushed their finished dessert plates aside and placed her phone down on the table between them. They began to flick through images, soon deep in conversation, their heads almost touching.

Both he and Georgie had returned to the villa after the hotel tour to change for dinner. When she had reappeared downstairs he had struggled not to stare at her as she'd joined him out in the villa's garden. The loose denim-blue silk blouse she wore was buttoned low, and a teardrop pendant sparkled just above the valley of her breasts. White palazzo pants hugged her hips, while her hair, tied up in a loose ponytail, emphasised the high-cheekboned delicate beauty of her face.

Despite his misgivings at the start of their hotel tour together—which hadn't been helped when Georgie had insisted that he had to inspect every female bathroom and spa changing room with her—she had made a number of useful suggestions. Including the addition of hair straighteners in the female changing rooms at the gym and the provision of extra fresh towels for guests using the daybeds on the beach who might want to swim on a number of occasions throughout the day.

She had also, following her briefing to some of the businesses in town, suggested that they showcase local arts and crafts in the reception area. But it had been her enthusiasm, excitement, and her belief in the future success of The Korinna that had taken him aback. Her optimism had lightened something in him. For the ninety minutes or so during which they'd toured the hotel he had started to believe that just maybe everything would be okay.

And throughout tonight's dinner, even though tension still existed between him and his brothers, Georgie's lightheartedness, relaxed and engaging style had made it...*fun*. It had actually felt good to sit for a few hours with his family and not focus on work.

Beneath a ficus tree they had eaten chargrilled squid and tender scallops with tzatziki. Their conversation had been interrupted several times by fellow diners, who had stopped to wish them well with the reopening, several saying how proud their parents would be to see them working together.

All four of them had avoided making eye contact with one another on those occasions.

Across the table from him he saw Georgie reach for Angeliki's hair and lift it away from her face. They were obviously discussing hairstyles. Angeliki's rapt attention never wavered from Georgie and his heart sank.

He couldn't allow Angeliki to grow too close to Georgie. She had adored his PA before Eleni—Rea, who had left the island after a whirlwind romance with a hotel guest and moved to Chicago to marry him. Angeliki had become withdrawn after Rea had left and then had proceeded to act out. She had been suspended from school, had constantly arrived home past her curfew time, and had started dating less than desirable guys who had been more interested in who she was and what they could get from her rather than in caring for her.

She was older now, of course, but she still had a worrying need for support and reassurance. And her taste in men certainly hadn't improved.

He leant across to Nikos and Marios, who were deep in conversation about Marios's most recent scuba-diving expedition, biting back the temptation to tell Nikos that he shouldn't be encouraging Marios's obsession.

'I'll get the bill.'

He waved away their objections and went inside to pay, trying to ignore the stab of envy at how close his brothers were and knowing how excluded he was from their lives.

When he returned to the table both brothers thanked him with a stiff formality more in keeping with the thanks they might give to a boss they'd had no choice but to dine with and left the restaurant together. Probably to head to a nearby bar.

If their parents had still been alive would his relationship with his brothers be different? Would they treat him as an equal rather than constantly being guarded around him? Or would his parents' expectations of him as the oldest son—

especially his father's—always have driven a wedge between them?

He was about to suggest to Georgie and Angeliki that he walk them home when Angeliki leant across the table, all wide-eyed, her mouth fixed in an *OMG* expression, her fingers twirling, twirling, twirling the jet-black ends of her hair.

'So, Loukas, tell me about your hot date earlier this week, when you were in Athens.'

Despite being disarmed by the way her stomach hit the floor, Georgie forced herself to smile, as though amused by Angeliki's playful question.

Loukas eyed his sister warily. 'What date?'

Angeliki's eyes were alight with mischief. 'Tuesday night at Funky Gourmet. A friend of mine works there. She told me.'

For a moment Loukas glanced in Georgie's direction, those intelligent brown eyes sweeping over her as though gauging her response.

Georgie tried to position her features in a professional pose. But in truth it was physically killing her to keep up the pretence of an easy smile when there was a lump of envy stuck in her throat.

Shifting his attention back to his sister, Loukas shrugged, 'It was just dinner with a friend.

Nothing else. I have no idea why you're even interested.'

Angeliki laughed and said. 'You've no problem interfering with *my* relationships.' Looking in her direction she added, 'Georgie, Loukas is always telling me that I date the wrong guys—he even personally took one of my dates home on his boat within five minutes of him arriving on the island.'

Shaking his head in annoyance, Loukas growled, 'He was drunk.'

'No, he wasn't. He had had a single beer on the ferry over here. And he was *hot*. Georgie, you should have seen him. He was *so* beautiful.'

On an exasperated sigh, Loukas looked at his sister gravely. 'He'd had more than one beer.' Then, his voice softening, he added, 'He should have had more respect for you. I'm not going to let you get hurt, Angeliki.'

'*You're* the one always saying I need to be more independent.'

'I want you to be more independent in how you live…in your career choices. You should have gone to university last September, with all your friends. But you insisted on staying here. Going out with boys who don't treat you well isn't a sign of independence.'

Angeliki's chin rose defiantly. 'At least I *date*. Unlike *you*.'

'Well, that's going to change... I've started dating.'

For a brief second his gaze met Georgie's, his eyebrows lifting as if to say *I'm still waiting for you to produce the goods* before he gave his sister a meaningful look and added, 'I'm hoping to meet someone who will help me to keep you in check.'

Angeliki flicked her hair back, her expression outraged. 'I don't *need* to be kept in check!'

Loukas threw her an incredulous stare. 'Who did you meet in Athens on Wednesday night, when you told me that you would be here—working?'

Angeliki pursed her lips, her gaze moving up to the string of lights hanging above the courtyard. Then she glanced back at Loukas, a look of rebellion in her eyes. 'Dimitris Fafaliou.'

Loukas placed an elbow on the table and sank his forehead into his palm. 'Please tell me you're joking—after the way he treated you...'

Angeliki crossed her arms and shrugged, refusing to look at Loukas.

Since meeting her, Georgie had grown fond of Angeliki, enjoying her easy good humour and enthusiasm for life. But Georgie had also glimpsed a young girl with a constant need for approval—a girl who could easily be hurt. Loukas had asked her not to interfere, but she had to say something—even if it annoyed her boss.

She moved closer to Angeliki and said, 'Angeliki, please don't let any boy hurt you. You deserve so much better. You're beautiful and intelligent, with a huge heart—don't allow *anyone* to disrespect you or treat you badly.'

Angeliki gave a reluctant shrug, refusing to look up, her attention now on her phone, her fingers swiping against the screen. 'I suppose...'

Loukas glanced at Georgie and gave her a slow, grateful smile. Her heart rocketed through her chest in relief. She smiled back...and there it was again, that something between them.

But then he looked away and leant towards Angeliki. 'You're not to see Dimitris Fafaliou again.'

For a moment brother and sister stared at each other. In comparison to her brother Angeliki was tiny in size, but she made up for it in defiance. 'I'm eighteen. You can't tell me what to do.'

A muscle in Loukas's cheek twitched.

He stood and glanced in Georgie's direction and said, 'We'll walk Angeliki home.'

* * *

Instead of going home, Angeliki insisted on join-ing Nikos and Marios at a nearby bar. Angeliki begged Georgie to join them but she took a rain check, tired after her long day and in truth, even though she understood that Angeliki was smart-ing after her earlier argument with Loukas, cross with her for not inviting Loukas too.

After they'd dropped Angeliki at the bar, they turned back in the direction of The Korinna.

Along the harbour front, which was festooned with bunting to celebrate the upcoming Holy Week, the restaurants were busy, and a light scat-tering of early new-season tourists were drifting in and out of the boutiques and souvenir shops.

Out in the harbour the wooden fishing boats bobbed in a light swell. She inhaled deeply, lov-ing the floral warmth of the mid-April air. Beside her, she could see Loukas's expression was tense.

She drew in some more air and asked, 'Are you okay?'

'Why wouldn't I be?'

Despite his terse glance she felt her heart kick against her chest as she heard the tiredness, the weariness he couldn't hide in his voice.

'I'm guessing being responsible for an eighteen-year-old can't be easy. I know I was a nightmare back then.'

He stopped by the harbour wall, at the junction of the road and the pretty laneway that led up to The Korinna and asked, 'In what way?'

'I thought having a boyfriend would sort out all my problems.' She gave him a self-deprecating smile. 'It took me a few years to wake up to the fact that boyfriends only added to them.'

He backed up against the hip-height white-washed harbour wall, his foot touching the cast-iron of one of the many cannons that still stood guard, relics of the island's strategic maritime position in the Mediterranean. He reached his arms back and flexed them tight as his palms rested on the stone, the movement emphasising his broad frame beneath the white polo shirt he was wearing tonight, with navy chinos.

'And now? Are you in a relationship? Do you date?'

His questions came out in a low rumble.

'I've come to the conclusion that relationships and I don't agree… It's like having a gluten intolerance, but for me it's a relationship intolerance. I end up with brain fog and nausea.'

Her skin prickled at the awareness of his eyes on

her. And he wasn't returning her smile or laughing at her feeble attempt at a joke.

'That's why you said the other night that you're not wife material?'

She tried to keep her voice cheery. 'Exactly. Talking of relationships—I have two potential candidates I would like you to meet. I thought you should start with meeting women who are already on the island. Katia Gogou is Human Resources Manager for the ferry company. She's smart and ambitious and she loves Talos. And Nina Fischer moved to Talos from Frankfurt last year—she was a partner in a private equity fund that was bought out, and she's running her own small fund from here now.'

'They sound like interesting candidates.'

They were... Why, then, did he sound so unenthusiastic about meeting them?

'Earlier Angeliki mentioned that you haven't dated until now—is that really true?'

His steady, potent, one hundred per cent male gaze met hers. 'I haven't lived the life of a monk, if that's what you mean.'

She tried not to blush, but there was an intensity, a dangerous sexiness in his tone that made her gulp.

'My life up till now has been dominated by work and family responsibilities…' He paused and hit her with another dark look that had her imagining him all hot and sweaty and naked. 'My relationships have been brief.'

She nodded. Scratched the side of her neck. Nodded again. Then she took a deep breath and asked, 'You mentioned before that you're not looking for love…but would it be a bonus if you found it?'

His gaze narrowed. 'I'm looking for a marriage of convenience and the opportunity to recruit a senior executive into the business—not love. My life is complicated enough with all my responsibilities—I don't have the time for or the interest in a full-blown relationship and all the complications that would involve.'

He sounded so certain, so emphatic. And for reasons she couldn't understand she felt as deflated as a popped balloon by that certainty.

In the distance she could hear the regular rhythmic trot of a horse approaching. Horse-drawn carriages and bicycles were the main modes of transport on the island.

She swallowed and said, in the best breezy voice

she could muster, 'Should I arrange for you to have dinner with Katia tomorrow night?

'Please.'

She nodded and asked, 'And are you going to meet your date from earlier this week again? The one Angeliki mentioned?'

'Her name is Marinella.' He waited until a white open-top carriage passed by, pulled by a regal grey and carrying a young couple who waved to them enthusiastically, before he added, 'No... Angeliki was right. Marinella's future is in Athens, not here. But my account manager at the dating agency is continuing to source candidates alongside you.'

She forced herself to smile at him. 'With both of us working on it you should have a wife in no time.'

She'd have no problem setting him up on dates, even seeing him married—right?

They climbed the cobbled laneway lined with terracotta pots brimming with pelargoniums and hibiscuses in silence. Halfway up, some of the island's elderly residents were sitting outside on wooden chairs, chatting amongst themselves. Their faces were lined after lives well lived, and illuminated by the lights shining through their open doors.

Loukas stopped and shook the hands of the men. Georgie followed his lead, and all the women pulled them both down into tight hugs. The last woman she hugged tapped Georgie's cheek fondly, and then said something to Loukas which Georgie didn't catch but that caused everyone else to laugh raucously and stare in her direction. Loukas shook his head and Georgie smiled back, at a total loss as to what was being said.

When they'd moved away she asked, 'What did that lady say? I couldn't understand her.'

They passed under a street light and she saw an amused glint in his eye.

'She said that you were very sweet…and that she hoped you were the same in bed.'

Georgie gasped. 'She did *not*!' She laughed. 'She looked so innocent.'

Beside her Loukas laughed, a deep baritone laugh that lightened something inside her. They made it to the top of the hill, both still laughing.

At the entrance gates to the resort her platform shoe caught against a stone and she tumbled against him. He put out an arm to steady her, his hand landing on her waist. Butterflies flew around her stomach at the warmth of his touch.

She pulled away and turned back towards the lights of the town and the sea beyond. A large cruiser was far out, heading in the direction of Piraeus. The chatter of the residents on the lane was the only sound.

'It's so lovely here. The air is different from anything I ever experienced before—it's light, floral… I feel as though I can breathe properly for the first time in years.'

'Talos is often called the island of fragrances.'

She turned to him, 'That's a wonderful way of describing it—and so right. I grew up in cities. I'd never realised just how freeing it is to live without air and noise pollution…and where my farmhouse is there's no light pollution either. At night the sky is dazzling. I lie on the ground and just stare and stare at it. A million stars stare back at me.'

Loukas smiled at her description. 'You're falling under the island's spell?'

She knew she should stop gazing up at him, stop itching with the desire to touch him, stop wanting to know if touching her lips against his would ease the yearning ache that was twisting inside her.

'I think I already have.'

Something flashed in his eyes, but then he stepped away. 'Why did you decide to come to Talos and renovate a property?'

His question was gentle, but it held a trace of doubt, even suspicion. They began to walk down the narrow avenue towards the hotel. It was just wide enough to take the island's horse-drawn carriages. Deliveries and guests who opted not to use the water taxis were brought to the hotel by carriage via the ring road that skirted the town and took a gentler ascent up to the hotel.

'My dad bought the old Alavanos farmhouse late last year, with the intention of renovating it.' She swallowed against the tightness in her chest and added quickly, 'He died just before Christmas, so I decided to go ahead with his plans instead.'

His hand on her elbow drew her to a stop. Even in the thick darkness of the pine forest surrounding them she could see the compassion in his eyes.

'I'm sorry.'

She nodded and moved away, feeling too raw and vulnerable to handle the softly spoken sincerity of his words. She was *not* going to cry in front of her boss.

She stopped when he called her name.

'Georgie… We've got that in common—wanting to fulfil our parents' dreams. You renovating your dad's house…me buying a hotel in Florence.'

'You're buying that hotel because of your parents? Why?'

'My dad promised my mum he'd buy it if it ever became available—he was penniless at the time, but my dad liked to dream big.'

Taken aback by his reason for wanting to buy the hotel, Georgie asked, 'Would they expect you to *marry*, though, just to buy it?'

'No, but I want to do it in their memory.'

For a moment Georgie considered arguing with him, telling him that it was too much of a sacrifice, but she knew about love and grief and how it compelled you to do things that others might question.

With a shrug, she looked at him and said quietly, 'I really hope it works out for you.'

Loukas's mouth twisted. 'So do I.'

'You don't sound convinced that it will?'

For a moment she thought he was going to answer her, but instead he muttered, 'It's getting late,' and walked away.

They swung down to the left, away from the main avenue, to follow the path through the orchard, where low solar lights guided their way to the villa. Loukas seemed lost in thought, and it wasn't until they entered the villa's walled garden that he spoke again.

'Losing a parent is hard… Sometimes I don't think I really understand how much it has impacted on Angeliki. I want the woman I marry to be a strong role model, to be strict with her, push her to achieve something in life.'

Georgie could understand why Loukas would want his sister to be independent, but after their earlier conversation about the boys she dated strictness was the last thing she reckoned Angeliki needed.

'I think she needs love and attention above everything else.' Standing beneath the portico of the front door to the villa, Georgie hesitated a moment before adding, 'It can't have been easy on any of you when your parents died.'

She'd been twenty-seven when she'd lost her dad. What must it have been like for Angeliki to lose both her parents before she was even ten years old? What must it have been like for all four of the siblings to lose both parents so tragically?

Loukas opened the front door. A table lamp in the wide hallway was already switched on, illuminating the villa's dark wooden stairs that reminded Georgie of all the Christmases she had spent watching Scarlett O'Hara sweep down that grand Southern staircase.

Her own Rhett Butler turned and eyed her darkly. 'Georgie, I appreciate that you're trying to help, but I *know* what Angeliki needs.' He looked at her for a long moment, his jaw working, before he added, 'In fact, I would appreciate it if you kept your distance from her.'

He'd what? He had to be kidding her!

'What do you mean, keep my distance from her?'

'Angeliki becomes too attached to people. I've seen it with past boyfriends, staff who've worked here. She gets upset when people leave.'

'I'll be on the island for the rest of the summer. In the winter months I'll always be at the end of a phone, and Angeliki can visit me wherever I'm living.'

Running a hand along the evening shadow of his jaw, Loukas arched his neck. 'Why don't you want to stay here on Talos permanently?'

How could she explain to him the constant restlessness in her bones? The need to explore? Not to belong to anyone or anywhere?

As a child she had learnt not to let others in—not to share deep intimacies, not to forge truly close bonds—because it was too painful every time she had to say goodbye to those people when her dad dragged her off to a new city. Yes, she had formed friendships similar to those she now had with Loukas's siblings, but she had always avoided letting them become truly deep and intimate. It was a habit that had stood her in good stead in the past, and she wasn't about to change now—especially with this Greek god who kept steering her off course.

'I love to move around—try new careers, new cities, make new friends.'

Loukas leant against the doorframe and considered her. 'Georgie, for someone who likes to interfere, you don't give away a lot about your own life. Why's that?'

She stepped back from him. And yelped when she stumbled into the shrubbery and encountered a particularly pointy Yucca plant.

She gave him a breezy smile whilst rubbing the back of her leg. 'There isn't a lot to tell. You get what you see with me.'

His sceptical gaze told her what he thought of her answer.

He jingled the keys in his hand. 'I have to go back to work. I'll see you tomorrow.'

She should nod and let him go, but the tiredness in his eyes had her reaching out and touching his arm. 'Do you have to? It's so late.'

His gaze moved down to her hand. For a brief second his fingers touched against hers. Her heart came to a screeching halt and then fluttered erratically back to life.

Soft, grateful eyes came up to meet her gaze. 'I have to. My acquisitions team are waiting for my response on whether to go ahead with a hotel purchase.'

In the few days she had worked for him she had seen the relentless pace at which he worked. Why did he do it? What was driving him?

'You work incredibly hard—why?'

'I'm the head of this family. It's my responsibility to ensure that the business is a success.'

She admired his loyalty to his family, but what must it be like to carry such responsibility?

'I know you told me not to interfere, but I have to admit how much I admire how protective you are of your family, how much you love them... even if at times you go about it the wrong way—'

Before she could say any more Loukas stepped

away, raising his hands in lighthearted self-defence, a cute smile on his lips. 'Goodnight, Georgie.'

Her bones melted. Boy, did he look good when he smiled like that. She didn't want him to go—not yet.

She called after him. 'Tomorrow morning I'm going to brief some of the businesses outside of town about the reopening. Stefania, who runs the jewellery gallery, mentioned today that there's a tradition of wood carving amongst the island's shepherds, so I'm going to visit some of them too.' Despite her bravado, and her best attempts not to overthink the goat situation, she felt a deep shiver run down the length of her spine as she admitted, 'I'm just hoping I can avoid any of their goats.'

Loukas made his way back to the front door, rubbing his hand against his jawline as though wrangling internally with a bothersome decision.

'I'll come with you.'

Really? 'I thought you'd be too busy working.'

'It's about time I visited some of my neighbours… I haven't done so in a very long time.' A cheeky grin formed on his mouth, and there was a teasing glint in his eye. 'And I can't have my PA being attacked by crazed goats, now, can I?'

They stood there grinning at one another.

She should say goodnight, go into the villa and close the door. But she couldn't. She wanted to be here, under the Greek night sky, with the sound of the Mediterranean in the distance, staring at Loukas Christou's wide, beautiful smile, at the evening shadow trailing over his jawline, the pull of his huge powerful body beneath that tight-fitting white polo shirt he was wearing…

His smile faded. The humour in his eyes faded too. To be replaced by an awareness, an intensity in his gaze that threatened to drag her forward, towards him.

Unable to breathe, she felt a fuzzy warmth spread through her limbs. And then her heart soared. He was moving towards her.

Gently he laid his hand against her hair. He came closer and closer and closer. The promise of his approaching mouth, his scent, the warmth of his touch was leaving her dizzy.

His lips brushed against her cheek. 'Goodnight, Georgie Jones.'

And then he turned and walked away.

Georgie, it was only a peck on the cheek. He's your boss. He's your neighbour and your friends' brother. You're his matchmaker! Get a grip. This guy is so out of bounds it isn't even funny.

She stared after him, dazed, putting a hand to her cheek where his lips had touched her now burning skin.

CHAPTER FOUR

THE OLIVE GROVES on either side of the steep track did little to shade them from the midday sun as Loukas and Georgie pedalled their bikes away from local farmer Vasilis's house. They turned at Vasilis's call to travel safely—*'Kaló taksídi!'*—and Georgie's bike wobbled towards his in the process.

Loukas reached out and placed a steadying hand against her back, feeling the cotton of her sleeveless white blouse warm under his touch. She wobbled away from him again, throwing him a grateful smile.

And once more something pinged in his heart.

What was he *doing* here? He should be at work. He should be returning Zeta's calls. He should be keeping his distance from his PA… For heaven's sake, he was going on a date *she* had set up for him tonight! This was crazy—especially how much he wanted to spend time with her, know her better.

He even had a crazy need to try and protect her. Which made absolutely no sense because Georgie was a distraction he and the rest of the family didn't need right now. A distraction who seemed incapable of not interfering in family matters.

But there was something about her empathy, her kindness, her openness to embrace others that touched him.

They had spent the past forty minutes sitting with Vasilis, in the shade of his porch, drinking *ellinikós kafés*, the thick and potent Greek coffee. Like most of his contemporaries on Talos, Vasilis was working long past retirement age—in his case, as a shepherd and olive grower. In his spare time Vasilis carved his own olive wood—exquisite miniature replicas of Talos's main landmarks: the lighthouse, the cannons lining the harbour wall, the abandoned fortress at Kiotari.

Georgie had held each of Vasilis's carved pieces as though they were priceless artefacts, marvelling at the minute detail, and Vasilis's pride and flirtatiousness with Georgie had grown more outrageous with each passing minute. Georgie had played along, smiling and gently teasing Vasilis, and Loukas had seen the spark that had been missing from Vasilis in the years since his wife had died and his only son had left the island never to return.

When they had finished their coffee Vasilis had tipped Georgie's coffee cup upside down on a plate and read her fortune from the leftover grounds. With a wicked glint Vasilis had declared that she would soon find love on Talos. Georgie had laughed at Vasilis's hopeful grin. But when she had glanced in Loukas's direction her eyes had darted away immediately, and a blush had blossomed on her cheeks.

Georgie was leaving with six pieces of Vasilis's carving, carefully wrapped in newspaper and sitting in her wicker basket alongside pottery, wood carvings and other artwork she had collected from artisans throughout the morning.

She was now further up the path from him, crouched over, pushing hard on her bike pedals against the steep and uneven incline. His eyes trailed over the curve of her bottom above the saddle. He gripped his handlebars tighter, pushed down on his own pedals more furiously.

Her hair was tied back in a high ponytail... Was it crazy to find the exposed skin at the nape of her neck so sexy? To imagine laying his lips there?

To inhale her? Taste her? Would she sigh? Shiver? Turn to him? Pull away?

He needed to stop this.

What had happened to his self-discipline?

He needed to turn for home.

Now.

He needed to focus on what was important: honouring his father's commitment to buy the Convento San Francesco and doing everything in his power to ensure the success of the family business. Both of which required him to find a suitable wife.

By her own admission Georgie wasn't interested in relationships, and even if she was Georgie wasn't what he needed in a wife. He needed someone truly committed to island life...a no-nonsense personality who would take his siblings to task.

At the top of the track they joined the main road that linked Talos Town with Kiotari, the only other major town on the island. Georgie crossed the road and came to a stop in the sheltered shade of the pine forest that ran along that side of the coastal road. The opposite side of the road dipped down to the sea.

The coastline here offered up tranquil coves, sandy beaches and ancient farmhouses like

Vasilis's, set amongst the olive groves that stared out to the tumbling beauty of the Mediterranean Sea.

Georgie fanned herself with the map of the island she had annotated with a list of businesses and artisans she wanted to visit. 'Gosh it's hot.'

She waved the map in his direction, playfully fanning him too.

'We just have the yoga and equestrian centres in Kiotari to visit now.'

She drew the map back to fan herself again.

'We haven't had much luck finding you any more dates this morning, but maybe we'll find you a sexy yoga teacher at the centre.'

He stepped a little closer. Leant down. Fixed her with a steady gaze. 'Perhaps. Or maybe we'll find one at the equestrian centre… I've always thought a woman in the saddle looks particularly sexy.'

Her eyes grew wide and her homemade fan fluttered faster, like the wings of a hummingbird. She turned away, tried to fold her uncooperative map and eventually just threw it into her front basket.

'Thanks for coming today…it's been fun.'

For a moment she paused and bit her lip, running a hand against the length of her neck. And then those hazel eyes met his and the vulnerability in them felt like a smack to his heart.

'My farmhouse is only a ten-minute cycle from here. I'd like to make you lunch as a thank-you… if you can spare the time, that is.'

He knew that he should say no. That he needed to get back to work. Back to the reality of his life.

But the whispering of the sea breeze, the lazy intensity of the sun, the nearness of Georgie Jones and the hesitation in her hazel eyes that told him her invitation had not been given lightly had him saying, 'Lunch would be good.'

Georgie's single-storey farmhouse, like Vasilis's, was set at the end of a dirt track off the main coastal road. Tall cypresses ran along the track, and corn poppies of brilliant red filled the fields behind them.

When they came to an arched pedestrian entranceway Georgie hopped off her bike and placed it against the pale stone garden wall. Even if she hadn't looked so apprehensive he would have known she was nervous, because she wasn't uttering a word. She opened the slated wooden garden door and gestured for him to enter.

She was clearly unsettled by him being here... so why had she invited him in the first place?

Inside, on the farmhouse terrace, an abandoned cement mixer and a lot of builders' rubble sat next to the old stone mill that would have once been used for pressing olives. Windowless, the house looked blank—as though it had lost its soul.

Georgie went and stood by the low terrace wall that ran along the front of the house, her hand running against the peeling paint of the wooden railing that sat upon it. With a low sigh she said, 'I'd forgotten just how much work there is still to do.'

He went and stood beside her. Steps from the terrace led down to a garden that had grown wild, and a path cut through it, leading to a small private sandy beach.

'Building work always looks worse than it really is.' He gestured around him to the work still to be done on the exterior, 'All this can be sorted within a week.'

She gave him a weak smile. 'Hopefully...' She gazed down at the garden. 'I spent almost a week clearing out the garden, but it doesn't even look like I've touched it.'

Then, crossing to a small wooden table and two matching chairs, shaded by an ancient olive tree and with endless views of the Mediterranean, she tilted one of the chairs and brushed some leaves off the seat.

'If you wait here, I'll go and get us some lunch. I locked all my non-perishables in my utility room,' she said, and gave him a wide-eyed teasing look, her nervousness forgotten for now, 'so don't worry—I won't give you food poisoning or anything like that.'

At the traditional wooden double doors to the farmhouse she stopped and searched the pockets of her turquoise shorts, her long legs dancing impatiently until finally she fished a key out of one of the pockets.

'Don't tell me that you locked the door when you have no windows?'

She turned at his question, puzzled, and then with a laugh shook her head. 'You're right... I suppose it's just habit. I've lived in some dodgy places in the past.'

He winced at the thought of her ever being vulnerable, living somewhere she wasn't safe, and followed her inside to see a large reception room with a carved stone fireplace. The room was empty of any furniture or belongings. It was understandable, with the house still incomplete, but the empty room stirred something inside him—concern for Georgie, but also the feeling that she was just passing through...not just with this house, but with this island, his family...even with him.

He followed her again as she disappeared through another door, this time into a large kitchen-dining room. New kitchen units in a pale cream shade and wall tiles in vintage Moroccan tapestry colours of blue and grey had already been installed. A metal patio table and two chairs sat in the dining room.

Georgie walked to the rear of the kitchen and unlocked the door there.

'This farmhouse is quite isolated. Don't you think you'll struggle, being so far away from people?'

About to go into the room she had just unlocked, she turned at his question. 'I'll have guests staying with me when I'm here.'

'What are your plans for the winter months?'

Georgie shrugged and turned back to the utility room door. 'I'll probably head to the Nordic countries this winter.'

Her tone was flat and lacking in her normal enthusiasm. For a moment he considered trying to persuade her to stay, pointing out the opportunity for her to organise walking holidays here during the winter months. But he caught himself in time. Georgie's plans were none of his business.

He inhaled some air and said, 'Why don't you show me around?'

She led him from room to room, explaining the changes she had made, what was still left to do. She had restored the original dark timber ceilings and the flagstone floors. Some walls had been removed to create larger, brighter rooms, and additional windows added to take advantage of the panoramic views of the glistening Mediterranean. In each of the four guest bedrooms, new en-suite bathrooms had been added.

They ended their tour in the last bedroom along the corridor, and then Georgie led him back out onto the terrace. There she tended to a bougainvillea with crimson blossoms, training new shoots back onto the trellis attached to the wall.

He picked up an empty terracotta pot that had fallen over, seeing a tiny crack on the side before walking over to her. 'I'm impressed with what you've done here. The villa will make for a great guesthouse.'

She turned to him. 'Do you really think so?'

'Why are you so surprised?'

She turned back to the bougainvillea and began to train more infant shoots. 'You own some of the most prestigious hotels in Greece. And look at the work you've done in The Korinna.' She paused, her fingers lightly touching against the petal of a blossom. 'I suppose I've been worried that I'm not doing justice to this house…that I'm not doing it right.'

The disquiet in her voice, and the fact that though she'd glanced in his direction it had been only for a brief second…as though to do so for any longer would leave her too exposed…made him ask, 'Right for whom?'

Georgie closed her eyes for a brief second. Why was having Loukas here in her home so unsettling? Even inviting him here had her tied up into knots of uncertainty that she hadn't expected. She *did* want him here, wanted to thank him for this morning, but for some reason sharing her home with him had left her feeling vulnerable and unsure and not in control.

She inhaled deeply before admitting, 'I want to get it right for my dad.'

For crying out loud, why is my throat so tight?

She walked away from the concern in Loukas's eyes and stood again at the entrance to the room they had just been in. 'I'm going to make this my bedroom… It will get the morning sun. It's large enough for a sofa too, so I'll have my own personal space.'

Loukas did not move from where he stood. 'What happened with your dad?'

She had spoken about her dad with her colleagues in Malaga, even with Loukas's siblings. Shared some of her upset and dismay. But there was something about the intelligence, the empathy in Loukas's eyes, in his voice, that sent everything inside her into a tailspin.

'He died of an aortic aneurysm.' She flapped her hands, as if that would somehow ease the pain inside her. 'I'll go and get us some lunch.'

She fled through the bedroom and down the corridor. In the utility room she grabbed some dried penne, a jar of pesto and a bottle of red wine.

When she went back out to the kitchen Loukas was blocking her path. When he didn't shift out of the way she had no option but to look up at him.

His soft, understanding gaze ate up her soul.

'Your dad would be very proud of what you have achieved here, Georgie.'

And then he lifted the pasta, the pesto and the wine out of her hands. Placed them on the kitchen counter. He turned back to her and in one easy movement lifted her up and placed her on the counter, between the sink and the temporary two-ring gas burner she was using until her utilities were fully connected.

'I'll make the lunch.'

She went to object, but for some insane reason tears blinded her momentarily. She tried to clear her throat silently but it came out as a croak. Loukas glanced at her but said nothing. She couldn't even manage to tell him where the saucepan was when he went in search of one. He eventually located it, along with all the other utensils he needed. Not once did he speak to her...demand anything of her.

It was this silent acceptance of what she was feeling that proved to be her undoing.

Loukas moved beside her to fill the saucepan with water at the sink, and his assured movements, his strength and understanding, sent a fat tear rolling down her cheek. She swiped at it, hoping he hadn't spotted it.

What is happening to me? I've never cried like this before. This is so embarrassing... But...but I need to talk. I need to tell him...

'My dad was living and working in Croatia when he first visited Talos. He phoned me on his first night here, telling me about how gorgeous it was. He said it was an island of dreams.'

She swallowed against the croakiness of her voice but there was no stopping the words that fell out of her.

'The second night he rang and told me he had found the perfect farmhouse he could renovate. That he was going to move here and open a cookery school.'

Loukas placed the pan on the gas burner and drew back to lean against the kitchen counter opposite her. And still the words spilt out of her, his soft gaze cracking something inside her even though her cheeks were hot with the embarrassment of being this emotional in front of him... her boss, and—okay, she'd admit it—the guy she wrongly fancied rotten.

I must look like a mess, with red eyes and blotchy cheeks...

'He was so excited... But that was my dad all over. He loved travelling, finding new places. It was only when I came here last summer that I realised just how serious he was. For the first time I thought he might actually settle somewhere permanently. Throughout my childhood we moved constantly. He always said that one day we would settle, but it never happened. I stayed with him until I was twenty, then we started living in separate countries because of our work. Last year he went back to Croatia, while the house purchase here was going through, to work out his contract as head chef at a restaurant in Zagreb and also to raise as much money as he could for the renovations. I spoke to him every day before I went to work…and often in the evenings too.'

She stopped as vicious pain punched a hole in her heart. Memories of the mundaneness of her last conversation with her dad, the fact that she had only absentmindedly told him she loved him as she rushed out to work, without any thought that it would be the last time she would ever speak to him, knocked her sideways.

Her mouth wobbled and she was unable to form any more words. She tried again…but her lips, her tongue, felt like marshmallow. A large rock was stuck in her throat.

Her gaze met Loukas's. *I can't speak. Help me.*

The pain in her chest gave way to astonishment when he instantly answered her call—standing in front of her, gently placing a hand on her knee.

'Take your time.'

She closed her eyes. His fingers tightened ever so slightly against her knee, and his thumb rubbed against the inside of her leg.

Her heart calmed. She opened her eyes to him and said, 'I had just arrived at work when I got a call from his boss in Croatia. She was barely co-herent. She told me he had died. I kept saying she had to be wrong...that I had spoken to him only thirty minutes before. I went into total shock... I still can't believe he's gone.'

'It's only been a few months, Georgie.'

Fresh tears threatened at the back of her eyes at the understanding in his voice, in his eyes. 'Does it get any easier?'

For a moment he looked away, and then he ran his free hand against the back of his neck, his other hand on her knee steady and solid and re-assuring in the face of the ache that was swirling inside her...in the air between them.

'The pain isn't as intense...but I'm guessing that the sadness will always be there. I suppose it be-comes a part of you, changes the person that you are.'

Her heart missed a beat at the loneliness in his voice. 'You still miss your parents?'

He glanced towards her and then away. He arched his neck. 'I was with my dad when he died. I wish I had done more to save him.'

Thrown by his admission, she scrambled for suitable words. 'I… I'm sure you did everything that you could.'

He dropped his hand from her knee. 'If I'd started CPR more quickly…got Nikos to call the emergency services immediately…who knows what difference those things could have made?' His eyes swept over hers for the briefest moment. 'What I *do* know is that three young children were left without a father afterwards.'

She reached out and touched his arm. His jaw tightened. She didn't speak until he met her gaze again.

'You can't blame yourself. What benefit can it bring? It won't bring your dad back, and I'm sure he wouldn't want you feeling in any way responsible.'

He shrugged in response and stepped back, tilting his head. 'Have you any other family?'

She could tell that her words had had little impact on him. She hated to see him blame himself unfairly—but then hadn't she always done the same over her mum's disappearance from her life? Logic and emotion often didn't merge when it came to the people you loved.

All through her childhood Georgie had felt embarrassed, somehow at fault for her mum leaving. It had even got to the stage when—to her horror now—she had begun to tell people that her mum had died. It had been easier than saying, *My mum went away on holiday to visit her family and never came back.*

And, stupidly, those feelings still lived inside her. Rationally, she knew that she was wrong to blame herself, but that didn't stop the giddy panic in her stomach.

She inhaled deeply and tried to answer Loukas's question coherently. 'My mum left us when I was seven. She moved to Costa Rica. Her dad was originally from there, and moved to England where he met my gran. Both of my mum's parents died when I was young… My mum went to Costa Rica after my granddad died to meet his family for the first time. She fell in love with a guy there and never came home.'

His eyes wide, Loukas asked, 'Are you *serious*? She never came back?'

'No.'

'She left her *seven-year-old*?'

The horror in Loukas's eyes was so great she felt almost compelled to defend her mum. 'She sent me a letter when I was fourteen, asking me to visit her. Explaining that she hadn't wanted to take me away from my dad. That she was sorry if she'd hurt me.'

'Did you go?'

'No. I could barely even read the letter. I just wanted to block out any memory of her.'

Loukas nodded at this, before asking, 'Have you had any contact since?'

'She contacted me after my dad died. We spoke…but it was awkward and horrible, really.'

Loukas's hand moved up and his fingers touched her arm. The gesture was matched by the compassion that filled his soft brown-eyed gaze. 'How do you feel about her now?'

It was a good question. Georgie still tried not to think about her mum too much—and was this *really* a conversation she should be having with her boss?

But his gentle understanding, his own surprising frankness, his acute perception and the unnerving closeness of him, the size and strength of his body, the heart-stopping effect of his touch, had her admitting, 'I suppose I feel sad, more than anything else. I've accepted that we'll never be close. I feel sad for my dad, especially… Though he pretended otherwise, and was fun and outgoing on the outside, he was never really happy after she left. Maybe he would have found happiness here on Talos.'

'You don't sound sure.'

'After moving and travelling for the best part of twenty years it would have been a hard habit to break.'

His hand dropped from her arm. Something shifted in his eyes. 'But don't you agree that, like any habit, it's possible to break it if it's something you really want?'

For a moment she was thrown by the intensity of his stare. Her heart thumped in her chest. Just as it had done last night when he'd asked her why she didn't plan to stay on Talos permanently. Was he asking her for reasons other than general curiosity? And why did she feel both thrilled and scared at that prospect?

She jumped down off the counter and pointed to the saucepan on the burner. 'The saucepan is about to boil dry.'

With a low curse he lunged for the saucepan, moved it over to the other burner and switched off the gas. He rolled his shoulders before turning to her. 'Let's forget about lunch and go swimming instead.'

Was he serious? 'Now...? Here?'

He shrugged. 'Why not?'

Georgie knew her mouth had dropped open, but it felt as if her brain was moving in slow motion. Only one thought was slowly filtering through her brain. He *got* her. This huge Greek god—the most incredibly handsome man she had ever encountered, whose presence alone sent every nerve in her body jangling—this loyal family man, her infuriating and demanding boss, for whom she was supposed to be finding a wife, *got* her.

He got her.

He knew even before she did that what she needed right now, more than anything else in the world, was to lose herself in the soothing coolness of the Mediterranean, where she could wash off all the draining emotion clinging to her skin.

She eyed him teasingly, her heart dancing in her chest. 'But you have no swimsuit.'

His eyes devoured that teasing glint and a slow smile curled on his lips. With another shrug he sauntered to the doorway and out on to the terrace, and with one nonchalant movement whipped off his wine-coloured polo shirt.

Oh, good God! What's he doing? That chest... those drum-tight abs... I think I need to sit down.

He stepped out of his moccasins, lifted his head with a lazy grin and said, 'I'll see you in the water.'

Ten minutes later Georgie stood on the terrace steps and watched Loukas swim out from the shore, his front crawl stroke strong and assured. She was going to brazen this out. Pretend that he was just one of her customers.

She pulled at the leg of her swimsuit and then, unable to stop herself, surreptitiously adjusted the bust of her costume.

Stop it, Georgie. What does it matter how you look? He's your boss and your neighbour. No more! Now, go and give him the same attitude you'd give Nikos and Marios.

She marched down the path and across the fine sand of the beach, trying to channel some cool-girl attitude even when Loukas turned in the water and watched her approach.

She sucked in her tummy, regretting too late

all those *galaktoboureko*—the custard pies she'd become addicted to since she had come to Talos.

She waded into the water, tried not to gasp too loudly at the chill and called out to him, 'I have swimming goggles for you to use.'

He laughed and waved her offering away. 'I don't need them.'

She raised her hand, holding the goggles up higher and called out, 'You will after ten minutes in that salty water.'

With that Loukas dived under the water, his huge body barely making a splash as he sliced through the sea.

She waited for him to resurface. And waited. And waited. Then she screamed when she spotted a shadow moving through the water close by. And leapt into the air when a hand grabbed her calf.

With a self-satisfied grin Loukas emerged from the water. 'Goggles are for wimps.'

She tried to give him an unimpressed stare, but that was hard to do when her attention was diverted by the sight of slicked-back wet hair, seawater dripping down the hard planes of a man's chest and the constant question reeling in her mind...

What is he wearing...? Could he be totally naked?

She tried not to look, tried at first to meet his gaze, but there was a lazy sexiness there that she wasn't able to handle. Then she tried to stare at his collarbone, but thoughts of laying her lips there had her eyes fleeing, and before she knew it they were trailing down, down, down, until she saw a dark shadow under the water.

Her eyes shot back up to his.

He smirked. 'My underwear...it can dry while we have lunch later.'

Georgie shrugged, flung his goggles onto the sand. She pulled on her own, ignoring his be-mused look—why did people who'd grown up by the Mediterranean seem universally to find the concept of wearing goggles amusing? Nikos and Marios were the same—and sliced into the water.

Let's see how cool and laid-back the boss will be after a hard twenty-minute swim.

Her initial uneven strokes soon gave way to a familiar rhythm, her earlier upset for her dad and her jitteriness around Loukas easing and even-tually disappearing in the hypnotic strokes, the caress of the water...and the reassurance of the constant shadow of Loukas, who stayed by her side, stroke for stroke, throughout her swim.

They followed the coastline in the direction of Talos Harbour until they came to a cove, where the deep water gave way to a sea floor alive with marine life. She slowed her strokes and Loukas did likewise, and eventually they floated towards the shore with small kicks, pointing out to one another the shoals of darting fish.

In the shallows they stood and waded their way onto the small beach of the cove.

Clear of the water, Loukas said, 'Great beach… I've seen it from my boat but never come ashore here.'

Georgie smiled.

And then they just looked at one another.

Drops of seawater trickled down over the hard, tanned lines of his face, over his powerful neck and into the crevices of his collarbone.

Her heart thump-thump-thumped in her chest.

His hand moved against her hair, pushing it back off her face. It stayed just above her ear, cradling her head. And then he was easing her towards him, the gentle teasing in his eyes quickly giving way to a darkness that melted every last vestige of sense and reason that she was holding on to.

Her chest bumped into his. And then her hips landed against his thigh. Hard wet skin, cool to the touch.

Her eyes locked on the light swirls of dark hair on his chest. Unsteadily, her hand reached out and landed just below his ribs. Her breath hitched.

What are you doing, Georgie?

Go away... I don't know, and frankly right now I don't care.

Loukas shifted, his body angling in even closer to hers. 'Georgie…?'

She lifted her head to his voice, parting her lips.

Passionate, searching, intense brown eyes held hers, and then with a low curse his mouth was on hers.

Oh. Oh. Oh...wow.

Her bones melted…her heart spluttered and danced and throbbed. And his warm tender mouth teased, caressed, and opened up a whole new world of desire and attraction for her.

She arched into him, every cell in her body desperate for his embrace. It took her a few seconds to realise that it was she who had moaned. And in response his arm had hooked around her waist and he'd pulled her into him so that she felt every hard edge of him while his tongue explored her mouth.

She lifted both hands. Placed them on his neck, her fingers moving up to touch the fine bristle on his jawline. She moaned again.

And she almost cried when he slowly pulled away. But just his lips. His body and forehead stayed touching against hers.

With a low groan he muttered, 'That wasn't the best of ideas, was it?'

CHAPTER FIVE

THIS WAS ALL WRONG. He shouldn't have kissed Georgie. He shouldn't be wanting to kiss her plump, soft, gorgeous lips again. And again. And again. And he most definitely shouldn't be wanting to pull her down onto the golden sand of this cove and kiss every gorgeous inch of that incredible body.

A very male urge to possess barrelled through him. Pleading with him to pull down the straps of her black swimsuit. A swimsuit that had been designed with only functionality in mind. And yet Georgie somehow managed to wear it with an oblivious sexy appeal that made it all the more sexy in his mind—it exposed the soft indents just below her hip bones, made the round fullness of her breasts visible beneath the stretched fabric.

He should move away, but some invisible pull kept his forehead against hers, his hands resting on the soft flare of her hips, his thumbs touching the edge of the fabric just above that soft indent of her hip where his fingers were itching to stroke.

Her long eyelashes, beaded with tiny drops of seawater, blinked and blinked and blinked. And those hazel eyes, full of brilliant greens and rusts, like some forgotten treasure at the bottom of the sea, were wide, as though she too was utterly dumbfounded by their kiss.

How could a kiss be so thrillingly new and yet so familiar? As though it was a kiss you had always known would some day come along and blast away everything you thought you knew and thought you wanted.

Georgie pulled a few inches away from him, wariness shadowing her eyes.

No wonder, with what he had just said: *'That wasn't the best of ideas, was it?'*

Despite his words he wanted her to stay just for a little while longer. He was liking her closeness too much, liking the tempting promise of what might be. So without much thought he added, 'But for something that wasn't the best of ideas... I have to admit it was pretty spectacular.'

Those dark lashes blinked again, and the wariness was replaced by a slow, teasing glint. 'I think you've broken your newest HR policy.'

He chuckled at the glee in her voice. This was exactly how they needed to play this. Keep it light. Accept that it was nothing more than a kiss shared between two adults who, despite how much they'd fought it, were attracted to one another. Nothing more.

'True…but you're only a temp.'

Mischief danced in her eyes. 'Maybe you should think of me less as an employee and more as your matchmaker.'

The idea of Georgie setting him up on dates after the kiss they had just shared felt absurd. But it was more than that kiss. The closeness he had felt for her in her house also made it feel all wrong. Her sadness over her father had touched something in him, and for the first time ever he had admitted his guilt over his father's death.

Now he felt torn about sharing something so intimate with her. Was he somehow making himself vulnerable to her? Was he letting his guard down too much around her? But it had brought a sense of relief to share those thoughts with her.

He decided to keep all those thoughts to himself. Wanting to keep this playful, and quirking an eyebrow, he said, 'That's quite a personal service you're offering, Ms Jones.'

'I aim to please—and now I can guarantee to any potential dates that not only are you a nice guy but you're also an exceptional kisser.'

He bit back a smile. '"Nice guy"? I think you can do better than that.'

'I suppose some might call you gorgeous—but you can be on the grumpy side at times, so we need to allow for that.'

He lifted his hand and gently rubbed it against the sand sticking to her cheek like glitter. Her eyes widened in surprise. She tried to speak but stopped, biting down on her bottom lip instead.

He cleared his throat, but his voice was still a husky murmur when he said, 'Stick with "gorgeous" and "exceptional kisser".'

She angled her head and he cradled her cheek against his palm. He should step back. Of course he should. But the ache in his body to press against hers was too powerful.

On a low sigh she said softly, 'I'll think about it. Of course we can never repeat our kiss… Kissing a client once for research purposes is okay, but after that I'll have to protect my professional reputation.'

His mouth shifted and floated over her. His heart thumped against his chest, and he felt dazed with the need to feel her lips again. Faintly he whispered, 'And of course you have to think about your intolerance too...or is kissing okay? Is it only relationships that you're intolerant to?'

'I have to admit that I'm feeling slightly light-headed...'

He moved his hand from her cheek to her fore-head. 'You *do* seem a little warm.'

The movement of his hand broke whatever crazy spell they had found themselves in, and with a roll of her eyes she stepped away and looked up into the cloudless blue sky, her arm reaching up to point skywards.

'I blame the sun,' she said

She twisted around so that they were both fac-ing out to the rolling surf of the cove.

They fell into silence until he said, 'This intol-erance of yours is pretty intense, isn't it?'

Her eyes met his before shifting away, and she raised her hand to brush at the last few remaining grains of sand stubbornly sticking to her cheek. 'I guess...'

He grimaced at the sadness in her voice and asked, 'When did you first realise that you had this intolerance?'

She shrugged and ran her hand along the opposite arm. Up and down. Up and down. Was the sea salt drying on her skin too?

'I think it was always there, but it became particularly acute with my first serious relationship... my only one, in fact.' Her jaw tightened and she glanced up again into the deep blue depths of the early afternoon sky. 'Alain was my boss, and the owner of the restaurant where I was training to be a pastry chef in Lyon. We dated for a while, but when Alain asked me to move in with him I panicked. I felt claustrophobic, as though I couldn't breathe.'

'Why did you panic?'

'I've spent my entire life moving around—I like the excitement and the freedom, the thought of settling in one place, committing to another person for ever, overwhelms me.'

He tried to keep his voice nonchalant, not sure why he felt so compelled to ask all these questions. 'This intolerance...do you think it's curable? Can you *ever* see yourself in a permanent relationship?'

She stepped towards the edge of the water, only briefly glancing back towards him. 'I like being independent. Being single suits me.'

He moved beside her. 'Why?'

'When I left I hurt Alain. I didn't mean to. I didn't want to cause him pain. But I realised that there's a toughness in me… It's not something I'm proud of, but I put my happiness before his. I dated some other guys after Alain and it was the same thing: I always grew restless and needed to move on. Basically, I'm not cut out for relationships.'

He stared at her, taken aback not only by how candid she had been in what she'd said, but also the solid resolve in the way she'd said it.

The water lapped against his ankles. He snapped a foot against it, sending an angry spear of water upwards, feeling thrown not only by her resolve but by the way the fierce competitiveness within him always to get what he wanted in life felt somehow thwarted.

He gritted his teeth. He needed to focus on what was the reality of this situation—Georgie Jones was nothing more than his PA and a matchmaker. 'So—why did you choose Katia and Nina for me to date?'

She turned and stared at him. Clearly taken aback. But then, lifting her chin as though readying herself for something she didn't particularly want to do, she answered in a gentle tone, 'Because they are both smart and strong woman who won't be afraid to question and challenge you.'

He sneered. 'The last thing I need is someone *else* challenging me—my siblings do that enough… What I need is someone who's tough and who will support me in the business and in getting my siblings to toe the line.'

She crossed her arms and looked him steadily in the eye. 'Aren't you tough enough on yourself and on the others already? Do you really need someone who will add to that?'

This conversation was verging on the ridiculous. It was time to end it. 'Maybe we should leave the matchmaking to my agency in Athens. This is all getting—'

Before he could add any more, Georgie interrupted him. 'I'd like to see you happy, Loukas.'

He was about to protest, insist that he *was* happy. But the words stuck in his throat. There was an honesty, a genuineness in Georgie's eyes, in her tone, that hit him sideways. It was as if she really, truly, deeply *meant* that she wanted him to be happy.

He stared at her, at a loss as to what to say. His heart smacked against his ribs. Again and again and again. Had anyone ever looked at him with such truthful affection and tenderness before?

Confused, unable to handle the emotions swirling inside him, he walked further out into the water until it was at waist height, and waited for Georgie to join him before they dived down into the turquoise sea together.

It was Thursday lunchtime and The Korinna had officially reopened its doors earlier that day.

The day had started pre-dawn, with all the staff attending a final employee briefing from Loukas in the conference centre. The atmosphere had been tense, but excited. The buzz in the room had felt the same as the adrenaline rush Georgie got every time she stood at an airport departures gate, part-excited part-daunted at the prospect of starting a new life in a new city, in a new country.

Loukas had kept the briefing short and to the point, his cool demeanour showing none of the tension she had witnessed in him over the past few days in the lead-up to the opening. He had been withdrawn, tetchy.

His dates with Katia and Nina had not been a success. And that, quite possibly, was the understatement of the year. He had texted Georgie half an hour into his dinner date with Katia, insisting that she join them in the restaurant, and she'd understood why when she'd got there. The normally bubbly Katia had been unable to string together any sentence more than three words long.

The following day Katia had admitted to Georgie that Loukas's dark good looks had reduced her to a gibbering wreck.

And then apparently Nina had spent their dinner grilling Loukas on the business. He had stormed into the villa after their date, poured himself a brandy and, when she had nervously asked how the date had gone, had growled, 'I want a wife—not an aggressive auditor.'

Georgie knew she should be disappointed—should feel some level of embarrassment and professional failing—but instead she felt a lightness because both dates hadn't worked out.

Which she knew was totally wrong. So she had thrown herself into the task of finding some other suitable dates, glad to have something to focus on other than replaying their kiss in her mind over and over again.

It was a kiss that they had both brushed off as being inconsequential. What other option did they have? Loukas was looking for a wife—in his words, an assertive career woman who would be an asset to the business. Qualities that Georgie, with the best will in the world, could never lay claim to. Not that she was in the market to be in a relationship anyway, never mind become someone's *wife*.

Today things had started off calmly. Loukas had stood in Reception, personally welcoming the first of the guests to arrive. But bit by bit cracks in the new systems and procedures of The Korinna had started to show.

Guests had arrived on their own private motorboats and yachts at the marina well ahead of the time they had been given when booking in, and as a result the water taxis at the harbour had struggled to transfer them all to The Korinna.

Georgie had rung for reinforcements from the water taxi drivers who had not yet started work, while Nikos had rushed down to greet the stranded guests on the marina and organised as many horse-drawn carriages as had been available to bring some of them to the hotel.

Then the hotel's Wi-Fi had decided to become sporadic in its service—much to the consternation of the high-profile journalists and bloggers who were attending the opening of The Korinna and unable to post to their social media websites.

Seeing what was unfolding, and realising that The Korinna was losing valuable publicity, Georgie had invited them all upstairs to the HQ offices, where they had full internet access and great photo opportunities for the entire hotel from Loukas's office balcony. Meanwhile the IT department had worked frantically to sort out the Wi-Fi access.

They had just fixed the Wi-Fi when the new check-in system had started to act up. Loukas had tasked her and a number of other headquarters staff with transferring the arriving guests to the terrace for refreshments and liaising with Reception to complete the required check-in paperwork, then escorting their assigned guests to their bedrooms.

Thankfully the guests had seemed oblivious to the issues unfolding as they were greeted and managed at every stage of their arrival. Everyone was in an excited, first-day-of-freedom holiday mode, and eager to see the renovated Korinna and spend time with family and friends over the Easter weekend.

Most of the guests—to a person elegantly

dressed, with immaculate grooming that spoke of wealth and pedigree—had seemed to know one another, and the terrace had been a perpetual round of handshakes and cheek-kissing.

The guests had seemed especially happy to meet Loukas. Throughout the morning he had remained in Reception, greeting each guest with a perfectly judged balance of warmth and professional courtesy. Only when he'd been briefed on the issues unfolding had he shown his exasperation, which had usually been with an unhappy stare in the direction of one of his unfortunate siblings before he had quickly given instructions on what needed to be done to remedy the situation.

Each time Georgie had arrived in Reception to escort new arrivals out to the terrace they'd all been slow to leave Loukas—the female guests especially. And Georgie hadn't really been able to blame them. Ridiculously handsome in a light grey suit that emphasised his powerful body, with his hair recently cut by the in-house barber, Loukas had looked like a Hollywood star walking the red carpet. And every time she'd spotted him, especially when he was smiling down at the female guests, she'd thought of their kiss...and how she would never feel his lips on hers again.

Now, after escorting to their room a delightful elderly couple from Portugal, Mr and Mrs Dias, who had first visited The Korinna to celebrate their silver wedding anniversary the year it had first opened its doors, Georgie raced back down the stairs to save time. But on entering the reception area her footsteps faltered when she'd seen Loukas and a dark-haired petite woman embrace.

The woman was touching Loukas's head, running her fingers against the closely cropped hair as though teasing him for having had it so tightly scissored. There was a familiarity, an affection between them that would usually have had Georgie smiling fondly at just how cute they looked together, but right now she just wanted to shout, *Hands off!*

She rolled her eyes at her own idiocy.

The woman was part of a large party, made up of at least fifteen others, ranging from an elderly grandmother down to the toddler crawling along the marble floor. Her daffodil-yellow dress was catching beneath her knees, but that didn't deter her in the least as she dashed towards the reception area fountain, with her amused but harassed-looking father giving chase.

Georgie stood to the side, waiting for Loukas

to hand the group over to her while he and the woman spoke at length. The tension in Loukas that had upped a notch every time something had gone wrong that morning seemed to have disappeared in her presence.

I am not jealous. That would be pointless and pathetic. I know the score here. Perhaps she would be a suitable wife for Loukas? She's obviously family-orientated. She's sophisticated and beautiful...

She gritted her teeth and scanned the reception area. She needed to keep busy, do something positive.

It looked as though she wasn't the only person feeling invisible—a teenage girl was slouched on one of the sofas, scowling at the group congregating around Loukas in between scanning her phone. Her whole demeanour screamed, *Seriously? Do I really have to be here when all my friends are off having fun elsewhere?*

Within five minutes Georgie had befriended the girl, whose name was Arianna. Having spoken to Arianna's parents and sought their permission, Georgie had then guided Arianna down to the hotel beach, where one of the hotel's personal trainers was holding a beach volleyball game for the teenage guests. She learnt from Arianna that the woman Loukas was speaking to was her aunt, Sofia Zisimos, a high-powered lawyer who had just moved back from Brussels to Athens. Most crucial of all, she was single.

Georgie made her way back up to the reception area, knowing she should encourage Loukas to consider dating Sofia but with every selfish instinct inside her screaming, *Don't you dare!* She was making for a pretty poor matchmaker. If there was an ethics committee in the matchmaking industry they would undoubtedly strike her off for unprofessional behaviour.

Exiting the lift at Reception, she passed a stressed-out Angeliki, who didn't stop as she told Georgie in one long, breathless sentence that the booking-in system was back up and running and the reception staff would be able to manage the few remaining guests by themselves.

With a pile of emails awaiting her attention, Georgie headed back upstairs. When she reached her desk she saw Loukas, making his way back out of his office, shrugging on his suit jacket.

'That didn't go too badly.'

He stopped and stared at her incredulously. 'Are you *serious*?'

She shrugged. 'It wasn't plain sailing by any means, but everything got sorted in the end.' He really didn't look convinced by her argument so she added with a smile, 'The guests are happy.'

'Well, *I'm* not.'

What was eating at him? Suddenly annoyed with him, with herself, with that stupid kiss that seemed to have changed everything between them, she said tersely, 'I assume these hiccups happen whenever a hotel opens.'

'Not in my hotels, they don't.' He moved towards the door. 'I have to go. One of the guests is unhappy with his room allocation. I told Angeliki to ensure that it was the one that he always requests, but she messed up.'

No wonder poor Angeliki had looked so stressed when she'd seen her downstairs. Loukas swept past her, his stupid big body that she still wanted to grab hold of and his self-destructive bad humour setting her teeth on edge.

'Let Angeliki sort out the problem with the guest by herself.'

He turned and looked at her as if she had just suggested that they get down and dirty right here on the office floor, in front of the entire HQ staff.

'Why on earth would I want to do that?'

'Because it's her job, because she needs to know that you trust her, and because you need to learn a little perspective.'

'Perspective?'

'Yes…you can't be personally responsible for every small failing that happens in all twenty-six of your hotels. Stop pushing yourself so hard.'

He placed a hand on his hip, and there was nothing light about those brown eyes of his right now. 'I have to.'

She stepped towards him and met his stare. 'No, you don't.'

He turned away and stormed through the open-plan office. Makis, the Christou Group's finance director, spotted him and walked towards him, waving some paperwork in his direction, but he detoured at the last moment, having seen up close Loukas's scowl.

When Loukas had swept through the double doors Makis threw Georgie a *What's up with him?* look. Georgie shrugged and turned back to her desk. She dropped to her chair and laid her forehead on the white lacquered surface of her desktop.

Why, oh, why can't you stop interfering, Geor-

gie? What is it about this family that has you caring about them so deeply?

Later that night, arriving home, Loukas found Georgie and Angeliki standing side by side at his kitchen island, both carefully lifting eggs out of a catering size saucepan and dropping them down onto wire cooling racks to join what looked like a legion of red-coloured eggs—at least two hundred, if not more.

The eggs had been coloured red with a dye created by boiling the skins of onions in water and white vinegar—a tradition for families on Megali Pempti, Holy Thursday—with both the egg and the red dye symbolising life and the resurrection.

On Easter Sunday—Kyriaki tou Paska—the eggs would be used in a tapping game called Tsougrisma, which had two players tapping the ends of their egg lightly against each other. The player whose egg remained uncracked won and, it was said, would have good luck during the year.

It was a game Loukas had played throughout his childhood with his family; he had been eighteen before he'd become the overall winner—much to the annoyance of his father, who had won every year up until then.

As though sensing his presence, Angeliki glanced up, her mouth tightening when she spotted him standing at the kitchen door. They had argued earlier over her room allocations. Angeliki had proclaimed that she had everything under control and that he didn't need to interfere. But he had refused to listen to her and had insisted on going to the guest's room to speak to him and his wife personally.

Angeliki had fought with him all the way up to the room, and given him a triumphant look when the guest had assured him that he was in fact now much happier with the room Angeliki had allocated to them—especially as it had a much larger terrace in comparison to his usual room.

Now, he stepped into the kitchen and nodded to both women, who silently followed his movements. He poured himself some water from the fridge before turning back to face their displeased gazes. He stared back, refusing to feel guilty for doing his job and frustrated that, despite his asking Georgie to keep her distance from Angeliki, she was not doing so.

He was frustrated with the endless crises they'd faced earlier. Frustrated by how much Georgie was getting under his skin.

He hadn't been able to stop thinking about that kiss. Even when he had met Katia and Nina for dinner.

Neither woman was what he was looking for—Katia was sweet but much too quiet, whereas Nina was even more of a workaholic than he was and had yawned when he'd spoken about his siblings.

Okay, so he'd admit it: he hadn't tried very hard with Katia and Nina. And Georgie and that kiss were to blame. Today, as Georgie had rushed around the hotel, full of smiles and welcoming chat for their guests, intervening and sorting out problems so cheerfully, he had been torn by the desire to pull her towards him and kiss her again and irritation because her calmness had mocked the seriousness of the problems they were facing—mocked his own exasperation.

Angeliki dropped her slotted spoon down onto a ceramic platter he hadn't seen in years and said, 'I'd better get home.'

Wasn't that the plate his mother had used every year on Megali Pempti, when she'd dyed the eggs with Angeliki? Where on earth had Angeliki found it?

Georgie, her slotted spoon hovering over the saucepan filled with red dye, looked at Angeliki in surprise, and then at him, her mouth twisting unhappily before she leant closer to Angeliki, her free hand touching against Angeliki's arm.

'But we're not finished with the eggs.'

Angeliki gave Georgie an apologetic smile before looking back in Loukas's direction. There was nothing apologetic in the glare she gave *him*. 'I'm tired…it's been a long and *very* trying day.'

Georgie tried to persuade Angeliki to stay but she refused. After she had left, he and Georgie eyed each other warily for a few moments. Then, waving her spoon at the legion of eggs sitting on the countertop, she picked up a cloth and a large bottle of olive oil and thrust them in his direction.

'Help me finish these—they all still need to be rubbed with oil.' Her eyes narrowed dangerously when he didn't move and she added, 'It's the least you can do, considering Angeliki left because of you.'

He wasn't in the mood for rubbing olive oil into eggs. Not after the day he'd had.

But, given the determined glint in Georgie's eye, he relented and took the cloth and the oil and stood opposite her.

He considered the endless amount of eggs before them. 'Why so many?'

'Angeliki said that your mum used to personally dye one for each of the guests. She wants to do the same this year, to celebrate the reopening.'

Loukas stared at the eggs, feeling a wave of tiredness and guilt sweep over him. He reached for an egg and began to oil it with quick rubs, cursing silently when he discovered the egg he had chosen was still hot to the touch.

He glanced over to Georgie and caught her eye. Was that a smirk on her mouth? He worked his jaw and flicked his gaze back to the egg.

'The guests are loving the hotel. The feedback on social media is incredible,' Georgie said.

He shrugged, his annoyance over all the calamities of the day overshadowing any positive feedback they might be receiving.

He looked up at the loud sigh Georgie gave.

'*Why* are you so hard on yourself?' she asked.

'I'm not.'

'You've just reopened a five-star hotel that people are raving about. A picture posted online of one of the maisonette's private pools has got over a hundred thousand "likes" already.'

'Yes, but we've had one disaster after another all day. Clapping ourselves on the back when we got so many things wrong is both ridiculous and shortsighted.'

Georgie walked to the sink and poured the dye from the saucepan down the drain, her movements quick and sharp, before turning back to him. 'But you coped. You coped as a family. You worked together. Isn't that what's important?'

He dropped the egg he was oiling and stared at her. She was right. His siblings had been proactive all day. But it had come too late.

He blew out an irritated breath and said, 'A lazy tailor finds his thread too long.'

Georgie's brows slammed together in confusion.

He picked up another egg and explained. 'Yes, the others were proactive today...as all three of them have been keen to point out to me. But they are not prepared to admit how their actions prior to today caused all the problems in the first place. If Nikos had delivered the renovation of the hotel on schedule we would have had time to test the systems. Marios should have ensured that *all* the water taxis were available from early morning. And *I* should have anticipated all the other problems that occurred.'

She shook her head and went to the warming drawer beneath the oven. From it she lifted a baking tray, and then walked back to the kitchen island, where she laid it down. She unwrapped the cling film that covered the tray to reveal a circular plaited *tsoureki*—the traditional rich and yeasty Easter bread flavoured with orange and *mahlab*, a spice made from ground cherry stones.

He stared at it incredulously. 'When did you make *that*?'

'Angeliki and I made it together this evening.'

He dropped the egg he was oiling, and the cloth. 'I asked you not to grow too close to Angeliki.' He swept his hand across the counter, over the dyed eggs, the *tsoureki*. 'This is the first Easter since my mum died that she has done any of this.'

'Well, maybe it's time that she did. And anyway, Loukas, she's eighteen. You can't say on one hand that you want her to be independent and on the other hand that you want to protect her from me... For crying out loud, what's that even *about*? You'd think I was a bad influence! I'm baking bread with her—not leading her astray with drink and drugs.'

'And what happens when you leave Talos?'

'Angeliki will know that she has my friendship wherever I go. Anyway, I'll be back every summer.' She turned and grabbed a bowl from a cupboard and cracked two undyed eggs into it. She picked up a fork, then paused, her eyes holding his, 'I'd like to think that you and I can remain friends too, when I leave at the end of the summer.'

He swallowed against the gentleness in her voice and nodded. *Could* they remain friends? Were they even friends now? Or was the awkward attraction between them always going to be a barrier against the truthfulness that any friendship demanded?

She stared at him for a moment, as though waiting for him to speak, but when he didn't she shrugged one shoulder, looked down at the bowl in her hands and began to whisk the eggs furiously.

'For what it's worth, I think today went pretty well, all things considered, and I think you should give yourself and everyone around you a break.'

'We can't become complacent.'

Georgie began to dab the beaten egg onto the top of the *tsoureki* with a pastry brush. 'I get that, Loukas—I *do*. But I hate seeing you being so tough on yourself. I get that you were made responsible for your siblings at a young age. And I know how tough it must have been—not only being guardian to three teenagers but also growing a business in the midst of a recession. But you have to stop some time and say to yourself, *I've done my best.*'

'But we're barely functioning as a family.'

'You're probably no worse than most families—especially those who are in business together. The architectural firm where I worked in Malaga was owned by two brothers. They fought. But the difference was that they trusted one another.'

'I *do* trust—'

Georgie interrupted him. 'You need to let the others breathe…to make mistakes and learn by them. Learn by sorting out their problems by themselves, not having you swoop in and take over. They need to know that you have their backs when they do mess up. You can't function as a family if there's no trust there.'

He watched her place the *tsoureki* in the oven, his irritation growing. He was feeling under attack, hating to hear the truth of her words. 'I'd trust them if they stepped up to the mark.'

She closed the oven door and turned and regarded him sadly. 'But you constantly undermine their confidence by second-guessing everything they do. You have paralysed them in their decision-making because they're so scared of upsetting you.'

Was she being serious? 'They're not scared of upsetting me.'

Georgie placed the bowl and fork into the sink. Then, walking back to the counter, she held his gaze and said softly, 'They love you…you're their big brother…and they're terrified of disappointing you.'

He gritted his teeth. *Why* was she insisting on interfering?

Then he dipped his head, taken aback by how good it felt to hear someone say that despite everything—despite all the arguments over the past few years—there was a possibility that his siblings loved him.

But then he lifted his head again, feeling righteousness taking over—a righteousness to fight the guilt of being a brother who scared his siblings.

'I have to keep us—this business—together. The only time they perform is when I keep them under tight control. This is what my parents wanted. For us to work together.' He paused and gritted his teeth again. 'My parents gave everything to this business… My father—'

A pulse was pounding in his ears, adrenaline was coursing through him, and words he had never uttered before, had refused even to think about, tumbled out of him.

'My father…his heart attack…he probably paid with his life to make this business a success. He worked relentlessly to give us this business—it was his legacy to us. And I'm not going to stand by and watch it crumble.'

For long seconds she stared at him. Then, not saying a word, she came and stood by him. Picking up a kitchen towel, she began to polish the eggs he had oiled. She polished one, and then another.

His heart slowly began to back down to its normal beat. And then she picked up another egg and met his gaze.

'Maybe this business isn't for everyone… Maybe Marios would be happier running his scuba-diving business.'

'As I already said, my parents wanted us *all* involved in the business.'

She shrugged slowly, her eyes gentle. 'Maybe they were wrong. Some people need to forge their own paths.'

He looked away. Then down at those damn eggs.

He dropped his cloth. 'I need to go back and check on everything at the hotel.'

Without missing a beat, with her eyes fixed firmly on the egg she was polishing, Georgie asked, 'Why isn't Nikos general manager of The Korinna? Don't you have enough on your plate in your role as CEO?'

'He's not ready for that position yet.'

Georgie glanced at him, and then down at the egg she was holding. She grimaced and ran a finger along a crack on the egg before gently placing it in the kitchen bin.

Straightening, she ran her hands over her hips, over the denim material of her jeans, and said, 'It's amazing what people can achieve if they know that other people believe in them. It's the same with Angeliki... She needs to know that your love for her isn't conditional on her doing what you want her to do.'

His hand shot out to grab the side of the counter. Suddenly he felt off-balance. Was he just like his father? Only showing love and approval when things were done his way?

He wanted to walk away, but the softness and understanding in Georgie's expression and voice had him saying wearily, 'I'm getting this all wrong, aren't I?'

She came back and stood beside him. Her hand went to reach for an egg but then slowly diverted and moved against his arm instead. 'You need to start trusting them. Accepting that they will make mistakes…and that you will too.'

Her hand was like a soothing weight on the fabric of his shirt. 'My father never allowed mistakes. His family motto was that the Christous never fail.'

She shook her head vehemently, the fine wisps of hair that had escaped from her ponytail bouncing with the movement. 'But that's not humanly possible!'

Georgie's outrage cut through the tension in the room and the core of steel running up through his spine.

He bit back a smile at the frustration sparkling in her eyes. 'He didn't think so. He was driven and ambitious and he worked every hour that God sent.'

She dropped her hand from his sleeve. Picked up the oiling cloth and handed it to him. 'That's where you get your work ethic from?'

He took the cloth from her. 'I suppose… We

were all expected to work in the business from a young age. I did love it—getting to know the guests, and in my teenage years scouting for new locations with my father. But he was a tough boss, with high expectations and endless energy, and he expected us all to be the same. The business and the family were one of the same thing in his mind. And I was the eldest son, so he and my mum made it clear that I had to protect both.'

She held out her hand for the egg he had just oiled and he placed it on her outstretched palm.

'You *are* protecting your family—nobody could do more than you are, and I'm sure your parents would be proud of you. But I think you're over-protecting them. You need to give them space and start to live your own life too.' She held her hand out to him for another egg, cleared her throat and said, 'I saw you talking with Sofia Zisimos today. You looked fond of one another.'

'Whenever I manged to get some time off work as a tcenager I was part of the same gang as her.'

Rubbing the egg in her hand with particular vigour, Georgie asked, 'Would you consider dating her?'

On paper Sofia was everything he wanted in a wife—ambitious, successful, tough, and she loved

Talos. Why, then, did he have so little enthusiasm to answer Georgie?

He shrugged and said, 'Possibly.'

Her eyes darted to his. She blinked hard. 'Do you want me to organise a date between you?'

'No, with the hotel being such a disaster zone I need to focus on that this weekend.'

He tried ignoring the voice in his head that said he could make time for a date this weekend if he really wanted to. Was he getting cold feet at the thought of marrying? Or was it his attraction to Georgie that had him feeling so unenthusiastic about the idea of dating?

He gestured to the workbench. 'I think we're finished here.'

They tidied away the utensils and other kitchen items they had been using in silence. Then, with nothing else left to clear away, they stared at one another. Why was he so reluctant to leave her?

He gestured to the door. 'I'd better get back to the hotel.'

She pointed at the kitchen clock, her head tilting to the side, her ponytail falling over her shoulder. 'But it's almost midnight.'

'It's our first night. I want to make sure the

dinner service and the evening entertainment went okay.'

She nodded. But then, her eyes narrowing, she stepped closer to him. And closer again. What was she doing?

One hand propped on her hip, she pointed towards his left cheek. 'You have some olive oil smeared on your cheek.'

He rubbed his hand against his cheek. 'Is it gone?'

She shook her head. 'No, over that way a little... no, the other way.'

She stepped closer and touched her fingers against his cheek. 'There...'

Her touch was gentle as her fingertips ran over the stubble just beneath his cheekbone. Adrenaline coursed through his veins, kicking against his heart. He stifled a curse. For a brief few seconds he reached up and took her outstretched hand in his. Heady sexual chemistry swirled between them. Her hazel eyes darkened as her body leant ever so slightly into him.

Pulling on every strand of willpower within him, he stepped away and nodded to her before he walked out onto the terrace, telling himself not to read too much into the disappointment shining in her eyes.

The fact of the matter was that once you stripped away the physical attraction between them they were two very different people, wanting very different things in life.

CHAPTER SIX

GOOD FRIDAY—Megali Paraskevi.

Leaving Loukas's villa as the setting sun battled the approaching night in a blaze of hot colours, Georgie made her way up the lemon-and-orange-perfumed orchard, inhaling the heavenly scent made all the more intense by the fading heat of the day.

At the top of the path she turned right for town. After a few steps, she stopped. Looked over her shoulder. Bit the inside of her cheek. And then, on a sigh, she turned around and walked towards the hotel instead.

The elderly couple from Portugal, Mr and Mrs Dias, were climbing on to one of the island's horse-drawn carriages when she reached Reception. She stopped and chatted with them, feeling a stupid lump forming in her throat when Mr Dias, with trembling hands, placed a blanket on his wife's lap, slowly and carefully tucking it in.

Next year they would celebrate their golden anniversary. Where would she be when she was their age? Alone? Content with that? Or wishing she had made different choices in life?

In Reception, groups of guests were mingling as they prepared to head out for the evening. Manos, The Korinna's concierge, moved between the groups handing out tapered beeswax candles.

Just inside the adjoining lounge she found Loukas. Standing chatting with Sofia Zisimos. Sharing a joke with her, in fact, judging by their wide smiles. And looking for all the world as though they had called one another earlier and decided to colour coordinate. Loukas's petrol-blue suit matched the stripes in the white and blue mini-skirt Sofia was wearing with a white blouse, open low. *Too* low, in Georgie's opinion.

Georgie did a mental eye-roll. When had she started being the style police? There was nothing wrong with Sofia's clothes other than the fact that they revealed a figure that frankly made Georgie green with envy.

Her problem. Not Sofia's.

Loukas turned and caught her staring at them. She dropped her frown. Attempted a smile.

He gave her a curious look. As though to say,

Well, what are you doing standing there and gaping at us?

He beckoned her over. 'Sofia, this is Georgie Jones—Talos's newest resident.'

After enveloping Georgie in her light spicy scent and a warm hug, Sofia drew back and clasped a hand dramatically against her chest. 'Oh, lucky you, Georgie.'

'You like it here?'

Sofia's grey eyes sparkled. 'I adore it. I spent every summer here as a child—my parents owned a holiday villa on the island, but sold it when we all left home. I haven't been back in a long time.' She paused and smiled up at Loukas. 'Now that I'm living in Athens I hope to become a regular visitor again.'

Georgie's gaze moved between the affectionate smiles Sofia and Loukas shared, and she felt her stomach twisting into tight knots. She forced herself to unclasp her hands. To relax. The Matchmakers' Union would definitely strike her off for conflict of interest when it came to her client.

She smiled at Sofia and said what any half-decent matchmaker would say. 'You should move here.'

Loukas's only reaction was a fractional narrowing of his gaze.

Sofia shrugged, glanced towards Loukas and said, 'I'm afraid there's not much call for lawyers specialising in EU Trade agreements on Talos.'

Georgie readjusted the white coat she was wearing over her black trouser suit and said brightly, 'You could think of a career change. The hospitality industry, perhaps?'

Sofia smiled politely, but with a hesitation that said she was wondering if Georgie had taken leave of her senses.

Loukas's narrowed gaze proclaimed that she most definitely had. 'Were you looking for me, Georgie?'

'I just wanted to let you know that I'm going to the Epitafios procession…in case you were wondering where I was.'

He studied her for a moment, clearly not convinced. 'Okay.'

Oh, just get on with it, Georgie. So what if Loukas accuses you of interfering again? The man needs some interference in his life. And this is ideal: a date and a family night for him in one go.

'Actually, I'm meeting Angeliki there—and

hopefully Nikos and Marios too. I was wondering if you'd like to join us. You too, Sofia. I'm sure you both have a lot of catching up to do.'

Sofia began to pull on the lightweight trench coat she had been holding. 'Thanks for the invite, Georgie, but I'm going with my family.' She paused as Loukas went to her assistance and held the coat for her. She smiled warmly at him and then turned and gave Georgie another hug. 'Nice to meet you, Georgie, and welcome to Talos.'

Georgie watched her walk away, feeling awful for being so stupidly jealous of someone so nice. She ignored Loukas's scowl and said, 'She seems lovely.'

Loukas worked his jaw. 'Yes, she is.'

She smiled weakly. She was playing with fire again, but she wanted him to spend time with his family. Okay, she wanted him to spend time with *her* too. But that didn't have to be anything more than two friends hanging out.

'Will you come to the procession…? All the others will be there?'

He eyed her warily. Fixed the knot of his navy tie that had tiny petrol-blue spots on it. Pulled at the collar of his white shirt.

'Give me five minutes. I'll let the deputy manager on duty tonight know that I'll be off-site for a while.'

The streets and laneways to the town's main square was bustling with islanders, young and old, making their way to the procession.

At the top of a narrow stepped laneway, alive with a rainbow of hanging baskets and terracotta pots filled with brightly coloured pelargoniums, the small boutiques and cafés along its length closed for the day, they caught their first glimpse of the square—packed with islanders, all holding candles that were glittering in the growing dusk.

The procession was already underway. The crowd were singing a low hymn, parting as the three carved wooden biers, one from each of the town's churches, carrying the Epitafio and bedecked in hundreds of stunning fresh flowers, were carried around the square. Priests followed, sprinkling holy water on the crowd, and in their wake the altar servers carrying candles and ornate gilded liturgical fans.

Angeliki, who earlier that day had joined other locals in decorating one of the wooden biers, had explained to Georgie that the Epitafio was a religious icon depicting Christ, made of richly embroidered cloth.

They walked down the laneway, silently watching the procession unfold before them. When they neared the end they came to a stop, unable to go any further into the square because of the crowds.

Georgie leant in towards Loukas. 'What a beautiful ceremony.'

He nodded his agreement, his eyes briefly meeting hers before he turned to stare back out at the sea of candles again. All the crowd were singing, and the uplifting unity of their voices touched something deep within her.

'It must be lovely to have such traditions—to be part of the same community all your life.'

Loukas had put a lightweight black coat over his suit before he had left the hotel. He placed his hands in the pockets of the coat, those beautiful brown eyes holding hers for a few seconds.

'I haven't made it to the procession in a long time.'

Gosh, he was… He was so handsome and beautiful and sexy and *so* out of bounds.

'Too busy?'

He gave her a noncommittal shrug and stared at her intently. As though he was trying to figure her out somehow. She looked away, suddenly uncomfortable. Suddenly afraid that she was going to give away just how much she was attracted to him.

She looked around at the crowd, her heart thudding. Knowing without looking that he was still staring at her. Her cheeks began to burn…

With a delighted yelp, she pointed to the one side. 'There's Angeliki and the others.'

He followed the direction of her hand to where his siblings were standing on the balcony of a restaurant with some friends of Nikos's.

She went to move, but Loukas's hand reached out for her elbow and pulled her to a stop. He moved in close to her. Dropped his head. She inhaled citrus, cedar, *him*. Her bones melted.

'If you stayed on Talos you could be part of all of this too.'

She closed her eyes for a moment. Overwhelmed by his closeness. By the gravelly sombre sexiness of his voice. By the pointless hope that flared in her at his words. 'I suppose…'

His eyes held hers, that soft brown gaze searching hers as though looking for answers when she didn't even know the question.

Loukas grimaced ever so slightly before he took

her hand in his and silently led her through the dense crowd, his height, his size, his dark charisma, easing a path for her towards the balcony. She got a glimpse of what life would be like, having this huge, gorgeous, determined and loyal man at her side, easing her path through life. If only she was brave enough to stick around, to believe that ultimately he wouldn't leave and break her heart. If her own mother hadn't wanted her, why would someone like Loukas?

When they joined the others up on the balcony, Nikos and Marios did little to disguise their surprise that he was attending the procession this year, while Angeliki, who could never hold a grudge, gave a squeal of delight and hugged him tightly, forgetting their argument yesterday, before drawing Georgie away to stand next to her at the balcony rail.

Nikos nodded in his direction before turning to talk to his friends from Athens, who were staying on the island for the weekend. Marios nodded in his direction too, but quickly shifted his gaze away to stare at the procession.

Loukas stood alone, needing some space and time to clear his head. Georgie's poor attempt at matchmaking him with Sofia earlier…her delight at the procession…the feel of her hand in his… Everything was mixed up. He needed to start getting things right.

Starting with Marios.

He went and stood next to his brother. Bit back the instinctive desire to ask him about work, about the preparations for the movie awards ceremony the following week. Instead, for the first time in too long a time, he looked at his youngest brother. Properly. *Really* looked at him rather than associating him with work and nothing else.

At twenty-three, Marios was not the teenager Loukas always pictured when he thought of him, but in reality a tall, handsome, wide-shouldered man. A man who hid himself well behind dark eyes and an inexpressive mouth.

Marios had been fifteen when their parents had died. In that year he had gone from being the exuberant and cheeky youngest brother who had exasperated and delighted his parents in equal measure to being a sullen teenager who refused to talk, refused to meet anyone's eye, refused to acknowledge that Loukas was his guardian.

Loukas had tried to reach him, tried to help him in his grief, but Marios had shut him out. And, frankly, Loukas hadn't tried hard enough to get through to him.

He cleared his throat.

Marios glanced up at him.

'How are you Marios?'

Marios edged away from him. 'I'll have an update about the awards ceremony on your desk tomorrow evening. The Athens office was closed today, but the main project managers are working tomorrow.'

'I wasn't asking about the ceremony. I was asking how *you* are.'

Marios lifted his chin and eyed him warily. 'I'm okay.'

'How's the scuba-diving business going?'

Marios shrugged. 'Getting busier all the time.'

'Good.'

Marios's mouth settled into a tight grimace before he looked away towards the procession, to where some of the crowd were passing beneath the biers in order to be blessed. 'You don't mean that.'

Loukas waited until Marios glanced back at him before he spoke. 'I know how much scuba-diving means to you. If you ever want to work at it full-time, then we can look at you taking on another role in the group—perhaps one that would free you up during the summer season.'

Loukas caught the blaze of anger that flashed in Marios's eyes before his usual indifferent expression took over. 'Don't you think I'm up to my current role?'

Loukas gritted his teeth and tried not to exhale loudly. Georgie was right. There was *zero* trust between him and his siblings.

He worked his jaw, guilty and appalled that he had allowed this level of mistrust to develop. 'You're doing a good job, and I'd be sorry to lose you. But I've come to realise that the scuba-diving business means more to you.'

Marios crossed his arms on the grey padded jacket he was wearing above faded jeans and asked, 'Why are you saying this now? All along you have insisted that we work full-time in the business after graduating, that we pull our weight. What's changed?'

The mistrust and cynicism in Marios's voice was hard to listen to. For a moment Loukas wanted to tell him just to accept what he was saying. He hated to be called out by his younger brother. His pride, his hatred of getting things wrong was rising to the surface too easily. But then he thought about what Georgie had said last night. That he had to allow himself to fail. That he had to allow the others to breathe, to follow their own paths in life.

He needed to start that process now. Start by admitting to Marios that he had messed up but they could move on from that. He cracked his jaw. Shuffled for a moment. The words were hard to find, hard to say, and hard to hear being said aloud.

'I've come to the realisation that there's been too much unhappiness in this family. I've got things wrong, Marios… I haven't listened to you all enough. It's time for us to be a family again— not just four siblings trying to run a business.'

Marios stared at him incredulously for a moment. And then, with a laugh, he shook his head, nodded in the direction of Georgie and said, 'Georgie's getting to you, isn't she?'

What the hell…?

'*No!*' Loukas could feel heat rising in him. Marios was staring at him with open amusement. Loukas fought the urge to walk away. 'What do you mean, *getting* to me?'

Marios's amusement appeared to go up a notch.

There was even a rarely seen smile twitching on his lips. He shrugged. 'Just saying...'

The crowd began to disperse as the three Epitafios left the square to be taken back to their individual churches, many of the islanders following behind.

Georgie and Angeliki, arms linked together, walked over to Loukas and Marios. Loukas stared at their linked arms and heard alarm bells ringing despite knowing he had to let Angeliki make her own mistakes in life, and even after Georgie's insistence that she would be there for Angeliki even when she left Talos.

Georgie caught his glare. Tightening her arm around Angeliki's, she let her gaze battle him, challenging him to believe in her, to believe in Angeliki's capacity to deal with what life threw at her.

A number of Nikos's friends came over and spoke with them as they left the terrace. Eventually it was only himself, Georgie and his three siblings who remained.

'So what happens from here?' Georgie asked with an expectant smile.

There was much shuffling of feet and avoidance of looking at one another before Angeliki answered, 'Most families go home and have a meal together.'

Georgie nodded, and smiled again expectantly.

Nikos took out his phone and stared at it, while Marios looked off into the distance. Hope simply shone in Angeliki's eyes.

Thanks to a disastrous Christmas Eve dinner two years ago, when he and Nikos had almost come to blows over Nikos's partying, they had all found an excuse not to have a meal together on a holiday since: skiing trips and house parties for his siblings, work commitments for him.

This family needed to change.

'Why don't we eat at the hotel together?'

Angeliki clapped her hands. 'Great idea!'

A frowning Nikos didn't seem so certain.

Angeliki rushed to his side, held on to his arm. 'You *have* to come. I'm not going to allow you say no.'

Nikos sent an appealing look in Marios's direction and looked confused when Marios shrugged and said, 'Come. We should celebrate the reopening of The Korinna as a family.'

Eventually Nikos nodded his agreement, albeit reluctantly, and then in unison all four of them realised that Georgie was backing away, giving them an uncertain smile.

'Enjoy your dinner.'

Loukas glanced at Nikos. His lips twitched. The same with Marios. And Angeliki. His heart soared. For the first time in years they were bonded in amusement—over the meddling but well-intentioned Georgie Jones.

He shook his head. Walked towards her. Tried to pretend that she was nothing more than a family friend, to pretend that he *wasn't* blown away by just how stunning she looked tonight in a slim-fitting black suit and kitten heels, her hair hanging loose over the shoulders of her white wool coat.

He forced himself to sound nothing but amused. 'Come on—you're invited too.'

And he forced himself simply to walk beside her as they all turned to walk back to the hotel, when in truth he wanted to hold her hand in his, wanted to hold her in his arms again, wanted to kiss those full soft lips of hers that were now beaming with delight.

Later that night, Georgie stood at the bottom of the staircase in Loukas's villa, trying to ignore the voice in her head.

You're all alone with him, Georgie, all six-foot-four gorgeousness of him, in this silent house. If you just reach out you can touch him…stand on your tippy-toes and you'll reach his mouth. Remember how good it was to have him kiss you… the explosions in your head…how intoxicating his taste was…how his teeth nibbled against your lip.

She tried for a relaxed voice. 'Thanks for dinner.' Okay, so that had been a bit high-pitched. She tried again. 'It was really lovely. And, imagine, work wasn't mentioned once!'

He fixed her with an unamused stare but his lips twitched. 'I tried.'

'The others all seemed to really enjoy it. Did you?'

Instead of answering her, as she'd expected, he frowned ever so slightly at her question. Eventually he said, 'Come and have a drink with me.'

He didn't wait for a response, but instead led her into the villa's main living room.

The square high-ceilinged room had blue-painted windows and French doors facing out towards the Mediterranean. A trio of luxurious white sofas surrounded an antique dark wood coffee table.

She removed her coat and sat when Loukas gestured for her to do so, and ran her hands over the white upholstery. 'Good job you don't have any children; these sofas wouldn't last long with sticky little hands.'

Without missing a beat, he answered drily. 'I'd lock them out. Confine them to their nursery. Now, what can I get you to drink?'

She cast him a sceptical stare. 'A white wine would be nice—and no way would you lock them out, I bet you'd be a complete softy when it comes to children.'

He shrugged. Took off his own coat. 'Would you like children some day?'

Something intense beat in the air between them. She thought about saying no. But there was something in his eyes, something stirring deep inside her that had her wanting to speak the truth.

'I'd like to, but given my wanderlust I don't see it ever happening.'

Loukas stared at her for five, ten seconds, his gaze unconvinced. Eventually he said curtly, 'I'll go and get our drinks.'

When he left the room Georgie laid her head on the back of the sofa and stared at the ornate cornicing on the ceiling. For a moment she placed her hand on her stomach, imagining what it would be like to have a baby growing inside her. To create a life with another person. A person who would stick around. A person who would love her with abandon.

She straightened up when she heard Loukas's footsteps out on the corridor and accepted the glass of wine he passed to her.

He sat opposite, close to the edge of the sofa, placing a tumbler of brandy on the coffee table.

'Maybe your ex simply wasn't the right person for you. Should you be ruling out *all* further relationships on that basis alone?'

Did they really have to talk about this?

'It's not just Alain, though. Before and after Alain, I dated other guys but it never worked out.'

Lifting his glass, he shrugged. 'But that's no different to a lot of people—maybe you just haven't met the right guy.'

'It's not the people I date who are at fault, though. It's me.' She grabbed a scatter cushion from the sofa and held it on her lap. 'I'm just not cut out for relationships. I want to focus on my guesthouse for now, and get to know the people of Talos. Have a fun summer. That's enough for me.'

'Is it?'

Oh, how she wished that he wouldn't look at her

so intently. That his softly spoken questions didn't feel as if they were pulling a protective layer of her skin off.

Thick emotion clogged her throat. 'It has to be.'

Annoyed by the scepticism in his expression, she sat upright.

'What about you?' she asked. 'Will a marriage of convenience really be enough? What about love and children?'

Loukas took a gulp of his drink. Dropped the glass heavily back on the coffee table. 'As I said before, I don't have room in my life for either.' And before she could argue with him he added, 'Why is making other people happy so important to you?'

Thrown by the sudden change in the direction of their conversation, she looked at him blankly before asking, 'What do you mean?'

'Take my family. You want to fix us. Why? You barely know us. We're not your problem. It's the same with everyone you encounter. I've seen how you've put Vasilis's carvings in the most prominent position in Reception.'

'You're my friends…at least I'd like to think you are. And Vasilis's carvings deserve to be sold. They are beautiful pieces of work.'

She stopped and thought of Vasilis, living out in such a remote spot all on his own, an ache for the elderly farmer twisting in her chest.

'Actually, I was wondering if it would be okay if I invite Vasilis to the Easter lunch here at the hotel. His son isn't returning to the island and he's all alone.'

Loukas rolled his eyes. 'You've just proved my point. You're constantly thinking about other people. You go about the hotel as though you have an inbuilt radar that picks up on people's moods. I saw you taking care of Sofia's niece Arianna yesterday, when they arrived. And today you spent a good half an hour talking with Mrs Hoffman.'

Cecilia Hoffman was well into her seventies, had a major crush on Loukas, and the most wicked sense of humour ever. Georgie's mouth twitched as she remembered Cecilia fanning herself when Loukas had walked by her in the terrace bar that afternoon, and her description of him as a 'bed bunny'.

'Her arthritis is getting her down. We were chatting about swimming and how it might help her.'

Loukas raised his hands in a *See what I mean* gesture. 'You practically glow when you talk about helping others…why is it so important to you?'

'You make it sound like I'm doing something *wrong.*'

'No, it's admirable. But at what cost to *you*, Georgie? Maybe you should focus on your own happiness too?'

Georgie drew the scatter cushion in closer to her, her fingers playing with the tassels along the edge. 'I'm happy.'

'Really? You can't commit to a relationship... You'd like children but can never see yourself having them...'

Georgie placed the cushion back on the sofa with a little more force than she had intended. 'Why are you making such a big deal about all this?'

Loukas ran his hand over his jaw. His chest rose and fell as he inhaled deeply. 'Because I care for you.'

Why won't he stop staring at me? She took a slug of her wine. *He cares for me? That shouldn't sound so significant, but it does.*

She dropped her head. Closed her eyes for a few seconds. Tried to clear her brain of the intensity in his voice, in his eyes, when he had said those words.

Because I care for you.

Words that thrilled her and yet sent a flutter of panic through her.

She opened her eyes. Reached for her glass. Found brief relief in the coolness of the glass against her fingertips.

'I suppose I've always liked helping others... Well, for as long as I can remember.' She stopped and thought back to some of her earliest memories—how she'd used to call in on their elderly neighbour Mrs Burton after her mum had left. Had run errands for her every day after school. She had loved the cosy warmth of her kitchen, the way Mrs Burton had allowed her to bake with her. Bakewell tarts on a Tuesday...scones on a Thursday.

'When my mum left, my dad and I stayed in Brighton. But a year later he was offered a position in a restaurant in Barcelona so we moved. For my dad it was a way of starting again. But he didn't settle—didn't settle anywhere, in fact. He'd stay eighteen months, two years in a job and then move again.'

She took a drink of her wine and realised that her hands were trembling. She stared at them in astonishment, then glanced towards Loukas. Her throat closed over at his sombre expression. At how intently he was staring at her.

She winced. She should stop talking. It was making her feel a little dizzy. But there was something in his calmness, in the way he waited for her to speak, that had her saying, 'Every time we moved I'd have to start a new school and make new friends. I found that the easiest way to make friends was to see how I could help them. That might sound cynical…it wasn't. I *do* like helping others, and it helped me too—to integrate, I suppose, and to survive. I'm an extrovert. I need people.'

'You don't have to help others, to try to fix whatever's wrong in their lives, for them to like you, Georgie.'

Georgie sat up. Her defensive hackles rose at how pathetic she sounded when he phrased it like that. 'I know that.'

In the silence that followed she bit her inner lip. Flicked her thumb against the stem of her glass. She was puzzled as to why her heart was hammering so much. Was her helping others *really* just about getting them to like her?

The image of her mum pushing her on a swing in the local park came back to her: her mum had been laughing as Georgie begged her to push her higher and higher.

How could she have walked away from that? Why didn't she stay for me? What didn't she like about me?

She dropped her head again. Ran a hand over the back of her neck. And jumped when Loukas sat down next to her, his knees almost touching hers.

'My guess is that in helping others you don't have to reveal too much of yourself. Because you're in control and the focus is on the other person all the time.'

'What? No! Why would I do that?'

Eyes that were much too intelligent held her gaze. 'I don't know. What do you think?'

What did she *think*? She had no idea, other than knowing that Loukas was hitting on some buttons she hadn't even realised she had.

'I think this conversation is getting way too heavy.'

He twisted even more towards her. She shifted away. Placed her wine glass on the coffee table. Crossed her legs. Heat was blooming inside her at having him sitting so close by.

'I've spoken to your builder, Sokratis. Your windows will be installed tomorrow.'

'Tomorrow? I didn't think he would be working.'

'I persuaded him to.'

Georgie would wager that Sokratis hadn't had a hope against Loukas; she had heard him on the phone all week, adapting his style depending on who he spoke with, charming with some, dogged with others. Always getting what he wanted.

Thrown, she frowned, not sure how she felt about him interfering in her house renovations.

'I've also told him to get extra men in there to get it finished by the end of next week. And I've scheduled interviews to recruit a permanent PA next week.'

He had...?

Her heart sank with disappointment...and then a rush of shame had her clasping her hands together. Determined not to show it, she angled herself towards him and raised an eyebrow. 'Are you trying to get rid of me?'

'You really don't like people helping you, do you?'

Was that all he was doing? Helping her? But

what if she was right and he did want to be shot of her?

Her stomach churned. 'No… It's… Oh, I don't know.'

His hand touched against her leg. 'I want you to be able to focus on growing your business— not worrying about this hotel, my family, moody teenagers, or lovestruck olive farmers with huge crushes on you.'

She swallowed. 'You do?'

Intrigued, and also terrified about what he was obviously trying to get around to saying, she stared at him. He flicked his soft brown gaze away from her. Worked his jaw. And then he turned back to her and swallowed her up with the smallest of smiles…a little hesitant, yet blazing with sincerity.

'I want to make sure that you stay on Talos for at least the summer.'

Lost for words, she nodded, shrugged, then nodded again. She laughed when his smile grew even wider. Yes, he was mocking her, but it was cute and affectionate. His hand shifted on her leg. Upwards. Her laugh died. Her heartbeat upped yet another notch.

His gaze ran from her eyes down to mouth. Darkened.

He drew in closer.

Her hand reached out…touched his biceps.

His lips hovered over hers.

Dizzy, she rifled through her muddled brain for some reason to stop this. In a bare whisper she breathed out, 'I'm your matchmaker…'

His lips touched the corner of her mouth. 'You're off duty right now.'

And then his mouth was on hers, playing with her, teasing her with featherlight barely there kisses that stoked the fire inside her to burning point within seconds.

CHAPTER SEVEN

ON SATURDAY MORNING, with his HQ staff on their Easter holiday, Loukas took advantage of the silence in the office to clear some paperwork and read through the quarterly briefings from his management teams. The financial returns were just about on target, but the property acquisitions were way behind schedule—in particular the Convento San Francesco.

Reading the reports, it became increasingly clear to him that he needed to focus all his attention on expanding the business—especially with the growth that they'd have to achieve in the coming years to remain a dominant force in the industry. Large consortiums were already sweeping up hotels throughout Europe and using their buying power to pressurise smaller groups to sell.

To facilitate the growth they needed he'd have to make management changes throughout his HQ staff. Which was why he had earlier called

Nikos and asked him to pop up to his office for a meeting.

It had been a tense meeting, with Nikos sceptical and wary. But Loukas had forced himself to be open with him, outlining the issues they were facing as a group and for the first time ever asking for Nikos's advice and opinions.

Initially Nikos had been reluctant to share his thoughts, wary of Loukas's motives. But as the meeting had progressed, and Loukas had shared his ideas for managing the business, all the time remembering Georgie's words about showing the others that he trusted in them, Nikos had come on board, often disagreeing, but at least they were talking.

It went against Loukas's management style and sense of responsibility to have to admit to someone else the problems within the business. For so long he had kept those details to himself, not wanting to burden anyone else. But talking with Nikos had helped him clarify his thoughts and plans, and—okay, he'd admit it—it had felt good to share some of the issues troubling him with his brother.

By the end of the meeting they had agreed that Marios would move over to be in charge of introducing new recreational activities to all the hotels, which would tie in with his scuba-diving business. Angeliki would remain as Front of House Manager, but they would encourage her to attend university, or alternatively to take on a deputy management role in one of their other hotels, or even outside the group, in order to expand her horizons. And Nikos would take the role of general manager at The Korinna.

Loukas had shaken Nikos's hand to congratulate him on his new role. Nikos had nodded, turned to leave, but then turned back. They had embraced awkwardly for a brief second. Both unable to look each other in the eye. They had years of quarrelling to overcome, but it was a start.

He clicked on his email. He would draft an announcement of Nikos's appointment and issue it next week, once he had briefed Angeliki and Marios.

There was a new message waiting for him from Georgie. He stared at the subject line: *Potential Candidates.*

He drew back from the desk.

Grimaced.

He hadn't meant to kiss her last night. But her honesty, her bravado, her vulnerability in talking about her past, her insistence that relationships weren't for her, had had him both wanting to protect and care for her, and yet to test her resolve. Which wasn't a great reflection on him.

He inhaled a deep breath. He had to face facts. He was developing feelings for Georgie. Somehow she had managed to bash through the wall he had erected around his emotions. A wall that had its foundations in his childhood tug of love with his parents. A wall that had grown to impossible heights the year his parents had died.

Having feelings for Georgie defied all logic. There was no future in what there was between them. He should be focused on getting himself a wife of convenience—a wife who would make no emotional demands on him. But when he was with Georgie logic seemed to fly right out through the door.

Their kiss had been slow and intense. Several times they had tried to end it, but time and time again they had relented, their touches growing more intimate each time.

Her deep gasp when his fingers had undone the buttons of her blouse and his thumb had brushed against the fine lace of her bra had stunned him into pulling away. At that point it had been either pull away or finish what they'd started. And he didn't even want to *begin* to think about how that would complicate everything.

This morning they had acted as though nothing had happened. Georgie was spending the day out at her house, gardening and painting. No wonder the palms of her hands were callused. He inhaled a deep breath, remembering the feel of those hands on his skin when she had untucked his shirt last night, their warmth, the slight roughness that had been so strangely thrilling.

He leant forward and clicked on her email.

Dear Mr Christou,

I have given thought and consideration to your requirement to find a suitable wife, and after a further search of potential candidates I would like to suggest the following:

Candidate One: Sofia Zisimos
Age: Twenty-nine
Occupation: EU Trade Lawyer
Association to Talos: Holidayed here as a child. Keen to return. May need to change profession.
Personality: Outgoing, socially connected, repu-

tation as a tough negotiator and ambitious—as reported in the Brussels Times.

Candidate Two: Anna Psarra
Age: Thirty-three
Occupation: Head of Marketing, Psarra Mineral Water.
Association to Talos: Family owns a holiday villa here. Sponsors and organisers of annual Talos triathlon.
Personality: Organised. Professional. Straight-talking—as described by Marios.

Candidate Three: Ourania Riga
Age: Thirty-one
Occupation: Head chef at Koozina Restaurant.
Association to Talos: Ourania has just moved to the island.
Personality: Ambitious. Likes to party. Talented chef. Hot—as described by Nikos.

Sofia and Anna are on Talos until Monday evening. I would suggest that you meet both over the weekend. I am happy to facilitate those meetings...although you can arrange your date with

Sofia direct if you prefer. I can organise for you to meet Ourania later in the week.

Trusting that the above is to your satisfaction, Georgie Jones

Loukas sighed. Looked up at the ceiling of his office. Rubbed a hand against the stiffness in his neck. Then he hit the 'reply' button and banged out his response.

As we've already discussed, I'm too busy to meet anyone this weekend.

He got an instant response.

You can make time. Which would you like to meet first?

He sent back a one-word response.

None.

Her reply was immediate.

All three are successful, ambitious and will stand up to you. What more do you want?

He stared at the screen. Only one answer to that question was looping in his brain. *I want you.*

He hit the 'reply' button again, all reason having left him.

Come to the midnight Easter celebrations with me tonight.

Her response didn't come for at least five minutes.

I'll let the others know that we're going.

He stabbed the 'reply' button.

Don't. I'll collect you at eleven.

A little after eleven, sitting at the top of Loukas's curved staircase, hidden from view, Georgie shot up when she heard the front door open and close.

Play it cool, Georgie. Don't overthink this. He's invited you to watch some celebrations. Nothing more.

Fanning her hot cheeks, she attempted a saunter as she made her way down the stairs.

Wearing a silver-grey suit, white shirt and black and silver striped tie, he lifted his eyebrows and a sexy smile danced on his lips as she neared him. His gaze travelled over the fitted bodice of her white lace dress, down over the flared skirt that stopped at her knee, and his eyes lingered for a moment on the ankle straps of her black kitten-heeled sandals.

She had bumped into Angeliki earlier and learn from her that Holy Saturday night was a night when people dressed up in their finery to celebrate this important holiday.

She popped her phone into the pocket of her black leather jacket for want of something to do, her insides burning up in the heat of his gaze as she remembered the scorching intensity of their kiss last night.

Still standing on the bottom step of the stairs, she went to move down but he placed a foot on the step and leant towards her.

'*Eisai omorfh*—you look beautiful.'

Her heart wobbled. 'Thank you...'

For crying out loud, Georgie, play it cool. Treat him as you would Nikos and Marios, with some teasing banter.

'You're looking pretty good yourself.'

His mouth twitched.

And, though she didn't want to, she forced herself to say the right thing. 'So, have you given any more thought to the candidates I put forward?'

His expression hardened and he hit her with an intense stare. 'No.'

'You should.'

He tilted his head and in that low baritone voice of his said, in an almost-whisper that somehow caressed her, 'I know I should, but I don't want to.'

With that he turned and picked up his coat, and two tapered white candles from the console table beside the front door. He opened the door and as she passed him they shared a look. A look full of acute awareness of one another.

Her heart somersaulted and anticipation zigzagged through her body in pleasurable bursts of energy, while her logical brain slowly shook its head in despair and said, *Oh, boy, Georgie, you're in big trouble here.*

In silence he led her to the church, which sat high above Talos Town. The small square at the front of the church was crowded. Through the open church doors she could see that it too was packed to capacity.

They passed through the crowd, nodding to those they knew. At the wall overlooking the harbour and the rooftops of the town below them

Loukas found a gap for them to stand in, his hand ever so lightly settling on her waist as they turned to face the church.

Without warning the square and the church were suddenly plunged into darkness. Beside her, Loukas whispered, 'It's time for the lighting of the candles,' and passed her a candle.

Slowly the church began to fill with faint glimmering lights, and then the priest emerged out into the square and in a slow-moving ripple a sea of flames filled the square as the islanders lit their candles from their neighbours.

Loukas lit his from a beaming older woman who patted his arm approvingly before he turned and held his candle out to Georgie. Their eyes met as his candle's flame ignited the wick of hers with a bright flash, and his hand on her waist tightened even more.

The priest re-entered the church and the crowd outside joined in with the prayers being said inside, loudspeakers beaming them out to the square. There was a soothing rhythm to the prayers and Georgie felt herself relax against Loukas, her hip leaning against his hard thigh.

There was a pause in the praying and then

the priest's voice called out joyously, *'Christos anesti!'* Christ is risen!

Around them the crowd began to cheer, and friends and families hugged and kissed. Georgie, taken by surprise by the jubilant celebrations, looked around her in amazement. The closest she had come to this kind of rejoicing was in New Year's Eve celebrations.

Beside her, Loukas moved. He drew her in closer while twisting them both round to face out into the harbour. He shifted again, so that he was standing directly behind her, his hands wrapped around her waist, drawing her back into his embrace.

A shiver ran through her.

She should pull away.

But it was too nice, too wonderful, too perfect. She'd allow herself just this moment.

She arched her back as his hand moved against her loose hair, tucking some strands behind her ear before he whispered into it, *'Kalo Pasxa.* Happy Easter, Georgie.'

His voice was way too sexy, his warm breath way too tempting. She arched even further into him as the open sky before them exploded in a multicolour blaze of glorious fireworks.

* * *

Later they walked home, following the candle flames of those ahead—a luminous sea filling the streets of Talos Town in celebration.

They carried their candles through the orchard, where the sea was the only sound reaching them. At the villa door he showed her the traditional blessing for houses in the coming year. Using the smoke of the candle he marked the frame of the front door in a cross.

Inside, they stood in the darkness of the hallway and she stared at him, watching the faint flickering of the candle dance on the hard planes of his face.

He blew out his flame. And then, taking her candle from her, blew hers out too.

They stood in the dark silence and she wondered if he could hear how her heart was pounding.

Thick, delicious tension whirled around them in the silence of the house.

She gasped when his hand landed on her cheek, his thumb running against her skin and then skimming over her lips.

In a whisper, she stuttered, 'I'm your PA…your matchmaker…we shouldn't be doing this.'

In the near darkness she saw him raise an eyebrow.

'True…and then there's your intolerance—we should be thinking about that.' His quietly spoken sensible words were negated by his fingers, which were stroking the sensitive skin of her throat.

She arched her neck. Her head was spinning with the need to have him kiss her again. Her body was aching for his touch.

He shifted so that his head was lowered towards hers. Into her hair he whispered urgently, passionately, 'I'm tired of pretending that I don't want you, Georgie.'

She let out an unsteady breath, her knees about to give way in the face of his bone-melting touch, the heat radiating from his body, the sheer size of him leaning over her.

She wanted him. She wanted his lips on hers. She wanted his hard body crushing hers. She wanted that beautiful mouth on every inch of her skin.

'I'm okay with brief flings…'

His hand on the back of her neck eased her forward while his eyes held hers, as though he wanted to make sure she was certain of this. And then his mouth was on hers, dominant and demanding. She answered back with her own desperation, her hands as frantic against his body as his were on hers.

Her body was pressed against his, and his hardness emphasised the soft, yielding curves of her own.

His hands moved to her breasts. She gasped at the shock wave that went through her as his thumb travelled across their weight.

And then he was leading her upstairs to his bedroom, guiding her to his bed, with the white walls and white linen illuminated by the bright moon in the sky outside.

CHAPTER EIGHT

ON EASTER SUNDAY morning Loukas stepped out on to the villa terrace from the kitchen, unease twisting in his stomach despite the blue skies and the warm breeze that greeted him.

He had expected to wake and find Georgie at his side. Instead he had woken to an empty bed and an empty house. She hadn't even left him a note.

Had she bolted? Was she regretting last night?

He inhaled deeply as a cinema reel of images from last night flashed in his mind and held him hostage—the sight of Georgie standing before him naked, all soft curves and delicious smiles. The fall of her mouth, her gasp, the astonishment in her eyes when they joined together for the first time. Her laughter and the sharp intake of breath later, when they had stolen out to swim off the small sandy cove beneath his villa…laughter that had shifted to low whispers and then silence as they had lost themselves in each other again.

After all that, why had she left him without a word?

Where was she?

He stalked back into the house, went upstairs to grab his phone and suit jacket, and was back downstairs within a minute. And in that time Georgie had miraculously reappeared.

Working at the kitchen counter, dressed in a navy and white striped T-shirt, cute cutoff denim shorts and a pair of pink flip-flops, she had her back to him. His heart kicked hard. Memories of his mouth trailing down the soft insides of her thighs distracted him from the fact that he was annoyed with her.

Her hair was damp. She must have gone to her own room to shower. Unease stirred even more. At what point during the night had she left?

She turned as he entered the room.

The initial disquiet in her eyes gave way to uncertainty and then a shy smile.

He came to a stop, suddenly unsure what to do. He wanted to hold her. Kiss her again. He wanted the laughter and closeness of last night. But hadn't last night been no more than a one-off between them?

But knowing something was one thing...doing

212 OF HER GREEK TYCOON

something was an entirely different prospect, and one that required a self-discipline that seemed to disappear whenever Georgie Jones was within ten metres of him.

He ran a hand along the back of his neck, attempted a smile. 'Are you okay?'

Her smile faded. She shrugged. 'Of course—why shouldn't I be?'

They regarded each other in an awkward silence for a moment. Loukas clenched his hands, knowing he should play it cool. But what they'd shared last night, the looks and the tenderness, were all too raw inside him, so without thinking he said, 'I thought you had disappeared because you regretted last night.'

She blinked. And in that moment he saw indecision in her eyes. But then just as quickly she shook herself, as though clearing her head of whatever thoughts and doubts were there.

'Of course I don't regret last night.' She gave him a smile that was a beguiling mix of shyness and sensuality. 'How could I when it was so great?'

Unable to stop himself, he muttered a curse, crossed the floor in record time and pulled her in to him, taking pleasure in how her soft body melted against his.

Pushing back her hair to expose the long length of her neck, he nipped the skin just below her ear. 'Where *were* you?'

Her body curved even further in to him. On a low exhale she said, 'Getting breakfast.'

He nipped her skin even harder. Her breathless whisper was the sexiest thing he had ever heard. *Thee mou!* She tasted good, smelled good enough to eat.

'Breakfast I can do without...you, I can't.'

She arched her neck, groaned low in the base of her throat. Her cheeks were hot, her eyes blazing with the same heavy desire that was pounding through him. They gazed at each other and a connection, a recognition of mutual need, beat heavily in the air between them.

Twisting around, she grabbed something from the silver breakfast tray behind her. She turned back to him and dangled a slice of mango in front of him. Slowly she bit into it, her eyes shining playfully. She chewed slowly. Toying with him.

'I thought you'd be hungry so I went up to the hotel kitchen and stole a breakfast tray while Chef Jean-Louis wasn't looking.'

She bit into the glistening piece of fruit again.

His eyes fixed on the sensual movement of her

lips, he warned distractedly, 'You're treading on dangerous ground. I've known Chef to ban people from his kitchen for far less.'

She reached around and held up a fat strawberry, bit her lip playfully and hit him with a sexy look. 'Trust me—you're worth it.'

He eyed the strawberry...her now parted lips. 'Today is one of the busiest days in the hotel...' He found it almost impossible to talk, as though he was drugged and trying to speak in a desire-fuelled haze. 'I need to get to work.'

But both of them knew that was not going to happen anytime soon.

He wrapped his hand around hers, holding the strawberry. He lifted the strawberry towards his own mouth and bit down on it. The sweetness zinged in his mouth.

And then his mouth was on hers.

Lifting her up, he carried her upstairs, determined to start the morning again. The way it should have started. With Georgie lying naked beside him in his bed.

She was late. Seriously late. She really should get going. But instead Georgie stared at her reflection in her bedroom mirror.

Popping her hands into the side pockets of her dress, she readjusted the fitted bodice so that the deep narrow slit at the front of the dress that ran from the base of her throat to the start of her cleavage was perfectly centred.

She had worn this knee-length rose-pink brocade dress and matching sandals to her colleague's wedding last summer. It was her favourite 'special occasion' dress. But would it be special enough for today's Easter celebration lunch at the hotel? Would its high-street credentials stand out for all the wrong reasons against the designer clothes The Korinna's guests always wore?

And then there was the matter of her hair. For the wedding last year her hairdresser in Malaga, Valeria, had styled it into a sleek bun. Unfortunately, no matter how many online videos Georgie watched, she had never manged to master styling her own hair, and now she was staring at her feeble attempt to replicate Valeria's creation.

She had pulled her hair back way too tightly, and now she looked as if she had had plastic surgery that had gone seriously wrong. And her bun looked like a beaten-up doughnut.

She rolled her eyes and began to yank out the clips. She flicked her gaze to the digital clock on her bedside table. It was one-twenty already. The champagne reception had started at one.

She dropped the clips on to her bedroom's dark wood dressing table, disquiet rattling through her.

What on earth had she done in sleeping with Loukas?

Last night it had been glorious and fun and sexy.

But when she had awoken this morning and stared at him as he slept panic had started to pound through her veins. Loukas was looking for a *wife*. She wasn't interested in relationships, and even if she was she wasn't what he wanted— a tough and ambitious career professional. And they were from different worlds. He was from the five-star luxury hotel fraternity, while she was from the rustic guesthouse brigade. He was all sleek and efficient…he owned luxury hotels and powerful motorboats, for crying out loud. While she was a tracksuit-and-hot-chocolate-following-a-swim type of girl.

Her temples were starting to throb. She needed to get a move on. But her hair, released from its bun prison, was now lying in a cloud of kinks and bumps.

She groaned out loud. Tried to run her fingers through her hair. It still looked a mess.

If her mum had stayed would she have taught her how to style her hair? Would she have created the sleek French plaits her classmates had often worn while she'd had one of her dad's lopsided ponytails that had always made her look a little demented? Would her mum have taken her for her first bra fitting? Shown her how to apply mascara? Listened to her sob over her first boyfriend even though it was she who had broken it off? Would she have been proud of her? Would her mum have loved her?

Georgie grabbed her hairbrush off the dressing table and yanked it through her hair.

Sleeping with Loukas had been glorious. He had been tender, attentive, slow…oh, so sensually slow…his mouth pausing at every inch of her body until she had begged him to hurry up. Time and time again she had lost herself in a world of pleasure and soul-searing connection with him, with their eyes locked together, silently acknowledging the enormity and significance of what they were doing.

It had all felt so right when they were in each other's arms. But afterwards, they didn't know how to act around one another.

This morning when he had been about to leave

for work they had both stood awkwardly in the hallway, neither of them knowing what the protocol was for saying goodbye to each other—he had eventually given her a chaste kiss on the cheek.

What was going to happen to them?

She twisted back the sides of her hair and secured them with two silver clips, leaving her hair hanging loose at the back.

She stared at her reflection.

Who was going to be the first to call for an end to this madness?

Across the terrace dining table from Loukas, Georgie and Vasilis both reached for an egg from the bowl of red Easter eggs that sat at the centre of each of the dining tables. Lunch complete, all the hotel guests were now participating in the egg-tapping game, Tsougrisma.

Georgie rolled her shoulders and placed her egg over Vasilis's.

Vasilis had looked uneasy when he had arrived for lunch, eyeing the champagne offered to him warily but Georgie had steered him in the direction of Mrs Hoffman and both widow and widower had got along famously, even though both only had broken English in common.

After the champagne reception Vasilis and Mrs Hoffman had joined this table under the canopy of the terrace, alongside Georgie, Marios and Angeliki. Nikos had also joined them, but was mostly absent as he was spending the day moving about the terrace and the hotel ensuring that all the guests were enjoying their Easter celebrations.

They had eaten lamb from the spit roasts that been turning on the terrace since early morning, salads and roasted potatoes with lemon, orange and oregano. The hotel's resident band were playing to one side of the terrace, and a light cooling breeze was blowing in from the Mediterranean.

Georgie shifted in her seat, looking for the perfect angle from which to hit Vasilis's egg. She glanced over to Loukas and smiled at him quietly, a host of different emotions flickering in her eyes: intimacy, affection, uncertainty, even sadness.

Aware of everyone else at the table, Loukas tried to keep his expression impassive. Georgie turned away and brought her egg down on Vasilis's with a gentle but defiant tap. She turned it over, examined it, and then glanced at Vasilis's egg. Both her arms shot upwards in victory and she smiled triumphantly before giving Vasilis a hug.

'Georgie versus Loukas in the final!' Angeliki called excitedly.

Loukas stood and walked around the table to Georgie's side.

'Watch him—he's a shark and hates to lose!' Marios swung back on his chair as he warned Georgie, his polo shirt the same shade of red as the Easter eggs.

Nikos arrived back at the table and, seeing who was in the final of their table's game, groaned. 'Do me a favour and beat this guy, Georgie—he's won every year for as long as I can remember.'

Georgie stood up and Loukas held his egg out to her. She eyed the opposing egg like a chess master. Her fierce concentration was so at odds with her modern-day princess dress, the clips that had slipped down the caramel and toffee tones of her hair. Her delicate rosebud mouth that had been so soft and expressive last night…this morning too.

He inhaled sharply at the image of her head thrown back, her damp skin against his.

Georgie glanced at him. Blinked. An electric charge ran between them. She dipped her head, a slow blush forming on her cheeks.

He cleared his throat…glanced at the rest of the

people at the table. To a person, they were staring at them with a mixture of curiosity and surprise.

He held his egg out further towards her, wanting to get this over with. No one could know of what had happened between them. Angeliki would only get her hopes up and his brothers, who were so protective of Georgie, would kill him. Especially as it was to be such a short affair. Especially when he had to marry someone else within the next month to secure the hotel of his father's dreams.

He gritted his teeth. Had he done wrong by Georgie? Should he call a halt to it now?

Georgie positioned her egg. Moved it a fraction and brought it down on his. He heard a faint crunch. Slowly Georgie lifted her egg. Examined it and then flipped it over to show him the hairline crack running down one side.

He held his up. There was no crack to be seen.

Everyone at the table groaned.

She shook her head and said quietly, 'I guess you're going to have all the luck this year.'

He glanced around the table. Wondered if he was doing the right thing. But he needed to reach out to her.

His heart began to race. He took her egg, placed

it on the table and handed his own to her. 'You have mine.'

Now she too glanced around the table, gave everyone all a tight smile before looking back at him. 'I can't take your luck from you.'

He held it out again.

She eyed the egg and then him.

He lifted his eyebrow, determined to play this cool even when inside he desperately wanted her to take this small offering from him.

Eventually she reached for the egg and nodded her thanks.

At a loss as to what to do next, with everyone at the table staring at them, he turned and grabbed Angeliki and dragged her out onto the dance floor, where other guests were already dancing the *kalamatiano*.

Late that afternoon Georgie walked back to Loukas's villa, keeping her head held high. She had had a wonderful afternoon. She really had. She had danced with Nikos and Marios and Vasilis. She had laughed as Mrs Hoffman had openly admired the dancing of the many handsome Greek men who had taken to the floor. She had circulated amongst the guests, ensuring that they were all having a good time, and posed for endless photos with the bloggers.

It had been fun.

So what if Loukas had kept his distance from her? It had been good to see him dancing with other women. And he had had a long conversation with Sofia—which was good. Wasn't it?

Inside the villa, she ran upstairs, undressed and hopped in the shower. She scrubbed her face clean of make-up and washed her hair. Humming to herself all the time. Needing to drown out her thoughts.

She was sitting out on the terrace, dressed in jeans and a short soft-knit jumper, reading a book and listening to music, when Loukas eventually came home.

He came to a stop close to the pool when he spotted her.

She pulled out her earphones in time to hear him say, 'You left the party early.'

It was an accusation rather than a statement. And she felt her hackles rise.

Before she could stop herself, she gave him a brittle smile and said, 'I didn't think you'd notice.'

He walked towards her, the spectacular red

sunset behind him silhouetting his huge body. 'Meaning?'

She stood at the coolness in his voice. And in that moment she stopped the pretence she had tried to maintain all afternoon that she didn't care that he had ignored her. That it didn't hurt that he'd danced with everyone else but her. That her insides hadn't twisted with jealousy at the sight of him and Sofia laughing together.

She angled her head. Tried to match his coolness. 'Meaning you were busy entertaining all your guests.' Despite the sickening feeling churning in her stomach, she forced herself to continue. 'And I saw you chatting with Sofia. As she is leaving tomorrow why don't you take her out on a date tonight?'

Loukas popped his hands into the pockets of his trousers and considered her for long, torturous seconds. 'I don't want anyone to know about us—that's why I didn't spend time with you this afternoon.'

She tilted her head back and shrugged. 'It doesn't matter to me.' Her chest felt as though a lead weight had settled there.

'You're upset.'

'No, I'm not.'

She backed away as he came towards her, but a raised flowerbed was blocking her escape.

His gaze was full of concern and frustration. 'If Angeliki finds out about us she'll make my life hell… She really cares for you, Georgie, and she'll drive us both crazy, trying to get us together.'

He was right. Of course he was. And even more importantly there was his need to find a wife. She didn't want anything serious with him anyway. But that didn't stop it from hurting so badly that she thought her heart was forming cracks, like those eggs earlier in the Tsougrisma game.

He stepped closer, and not for the first time she grew dizzy at his size, at his scent, at the intimate knowledge she now possessed of just how magnificent his body was.

He looped a finger in the band of her jumper and twisted it and pulled her towards him. 'You looked truly beautiful today.'

When he whispered like that he could melt steel.

She resisted the temptation to drop her forehead to the comfort of his chest and said instead, 'What about Sofia?'

Instead of moving away, as she'd hoped he would, Loukas pulled her closer, his hand reaching up to cup her cheek. Her heart did a triple flip.

In the barest of whispers, he muttered, 'I know we shouldn't, but I want to be with you again tonight…but only if it's what you want too.'

And then his lips touched against hers in the most tender gesture she'd ever received.

Her knees were about to give way. 'You're supposed to be focused on finding a wife.'

His teeth nibbled the lobe of her ear for a brief moment. 'We can go to my bedroom, or lie on the daybed under the pergola.'

Focus, Georgie. Don't allow yourself to drown in the testosterone oozing from him. If he's too blind to see it for himself, then as his matchmaker you're ethically obliged to point out that there are way more suitable women for him to be whispering these words to.

'Sofia's legal mind would be a huge asset to the business.'

'I want to slide your jeans off, have those incredible legs of yours wrapped around me again. The first time I saw you, when you cycled past in that mermaid outfit, it was your legs that got to me…that and your silver bikini top.'

He walked backwards, tugging her with him.

They shouldn't be doing this.

When he dropped her onto the daybed she tried

to point that out, but she was too dizzy from his nearness, too weak with longing, too dumbstruck by the intensity of his gaze as he hovered over her.

He tilted his head. 'Do you want this, Georgie?'

Her body was on fire, but heavy emotion—emotion she wasn't supposed to be feeling—clogged her throat.

She nodded, but Loukas kept on staring at her, waiting for her to speak.

She dragged in some air and whispered up to him, 'Yes… Yes, I want to be with you.'

CHAPTER NINE

'THE HOTEL WILL lose its sparkle when you three gorgeous ladies leave.'

The trio of female bloggers giggled at Nikos while fanning themselves with their checkout paperwork like modern geisha girls.

Beside Georgie, Arianna sighed. 'Nikos is so *cute.*'

Lifting her phone Arianna snapped Nikos and the girls, who were pulling playful faces as they posed for a group selfie.

'All my friends have fallen in love with the photos of him I've posted online.'

Georgie rolled her eyes. Nikos, with all his cheeky charm and dark Mediterranean good looks, would almost single-handedly guarantee The Korinna's ongoing success.

The reception area was hectic with guests checking out after the long weekend, most having availed themselves of the late checkout that the hotel offered.

From across the reception area Loukas, who was speaking to Mr and Mrs Dias, beckoned her over.

Once again he was impeccably dressed, today in a dark navy suit with a thin sky-blue pinstripe that was a perfect match for the sky-blue shirt he had paired with a navy tie.

The smile on his lips was a public one, for all the world to see and appreciate, but as she neared him something private and personal and just for her flashed in his eyes. Was he remembering their lovemaking last night? The urgency and the searing need that had had them whispering intimate words until only gasps remained?

Her steps towards him slowed and her pulse pounded in her ears. She tried to ignore the twitch of his lips as his gaze swept over the burning red-hot heat in her cheeks. She glanced away, and her heart slammed to a stop when she spotted Nikos, Angeliki and Sofia, standing in a group together by the fountain. They were staring in her direction and then towards Loukas.

Angeliki was smiling widely, Nikos was scowling suspiciously and Sofia looked…crestfallen.

Her steps faltered. Loukas's gaze narrowed and

then he turned to look to the side. His smile vanished when he spotted the other three.

Georgie wanted to walk away. She didn't want to hurt Angeliki or Sofia. She didn't want any friction between herself and Nikos. And most of all she didn't want Loukas scowling as he was doing right now.

A wave of guilt and shame swept through her at the role she had played in all of this, but there was also a brutal, sickening feeling of rejection at Loukas's determination to keep what they had secret from everyone.

Avoiding looking directly at Loukas, she turned her attention to Mr and Mrs Dias. The couple were speaking to each other in rapid whispers, interspersed with puzzled looks in Loukas's direction.

Eventually she had no option but to meet Loukas's gaze.

In a low voice he said, 'Will you explain to Mr and Mrs Dias in Portuguese that I would like to invite them back next year to celebrate their golden wedding anniversary, compliments of my family?' He pulled back and frowned. 'I think we're misunderstanding one another at the moment, thanks to my poor Portuguese. They think I'm asking if I can visit them in Portugal.'

In other circumstances Georgie would have giggled at the misunderstanding, but instead her heart sank as she watched Loukas move away to speak to other departing guests, clearly wanting to get away from her and any suspicions the others might have about their relationship.

She translated Loukas's generous invitation to the couple, who turned towards each other in amazement and then in unison hugged her before crossing the reception area to go and thank Loukas.

For a moment Georgie stood alone, feeling awkward and exposed. For a brief moment Loukas looked in her direction as Mrs Dias hugged him, but he quickly looked away again.

In need of a diversion she walked outside and waited for Mr and Mrs Dias to join her at their waiting carriage.

Before Mrs Dias climbed on board she hugged Georgie one more time. 'We'll see you next year, Georgie?'

Georgie hesitated for a moment, thrown first by an image of herself on the ferry, leaving Talos at the end of this summer, and then by the prospect of returning next summer to meet Loukas's new wife.

'I'm not sure of my plans...' She paused and swallowed against the confusion clogging her throat. 'But hopefully we'll meet again at some point.'

Mrs Dias considered her for a moment with quiet solemnity. 'You and Loukas—you're good together.'

Mrs Dias's certainty and the wisdom in her eyes startled Georgie. She shook her head and laughed. 'We're just friends, Mrs Dias.'

Laying her hand on Georgie's arm, Mrs Dias said gently, *'Só há uma felicidade na vida: amar e ser amado.'*

Georgie stood and waved the couple off, the translation of Mrs Dias's words echoing in her mind. *There is only one happiness in life: to love and be loved.*

She closed her eyes and shook her head, trying to get rid of Mrs Dias words. She *was* happy—she had friends, she had her travel and the promise of so many new cities and jobs and friendships to find and explore.

She returned to the now almost empty reception

area, but her steps faltered when she saw Loukas talking to Sofia.

There was none of the laughter and ease that had been between them up till now, and Sofia gave Loukas only the briefest of hugs before she turned away.

Sofia came to a standstill when she saw Georgie standing behind her. They smiled awkwardly at one another before Sofia quickly made her way to the elevators that would take her down to the beach dockside and the waiting water taxis.

Loukas came and stood beside her. As Sofia went into the elevator she looked back towards Loukas for a moment, with a wistful expression.

Georgie winced. She had messed everything up. For Sofia. For Loukas.

The doors of the elevator glided shut.

'Is Sofia upset?'

His gaze met hers for a brief moment before he looked away and spoke. 'I'm free for the rest of the afternoon. Let's cycle out to your house. I'll help you finish clearing the garden.'

Why hadn't he answered her question? Was seeing Sofia leave bringing him back to the reality of what they had done?

She shrugged and said quietly, 'I'll go by myself. I'm sure there's a lot of work you need to do here.'

Loukas frowned at her. 'I want to help you.' He stepped away, gestured to the management offices located to the rear of Reception and added, 'I just need to speak to Nikos before we leave. I'll see you at the villa in half an hour.'

Before he had a chance to walk away she placed her hand on his arm and said, quietly but vehemently, 'No, I want to go to my house *by myself.*'

She clinched her hands against the panic rising up inside her. She had got all this so wrong. She shouldn't have grown so close to Loukas. She shouldn't have slept with him. Now she just felt vulnerable and exposed and guilty.

Before he had a chance to argue with her she walked away, trying to resist the urge to run as she stepped outside under the canopy.

'What's going on between you and Georgie?'

Watching Georgie disappear out of the building, Loukas gritted his teeth and turned to Nikos, who was staring at him unhappily.

Was his messed-up relationship with Georgie going to cause a rift between him and Nikos just as they were starting to mend their own relationship?

He turned and stared out at the now empty hotel entranceway, his gut tightening after Georgie's refusal to let him join her today. He had seen it in her eyes when she'd said she wanted to go to her house by herself—she was pushing him away.

'We need to go through the financials for the weekend.'

Without waiting for a response he marched away and into Nikos's office, which sat to the rear of the reception.

He sat in the visitor's chair and Nikos sat opposite him, fixing him with a cold-eyed glare. 'Why's Georgie upset?'

'What do you mean?'

'Just now—before she left—she was upset.'

'Can we talk about the figures?'

Nikos leant back in his chair. 'Not until you tell me what's going on between you two.'

'Nothing's going on.'

Nikos shrugged and ran his palm over the wooden surface of his desk—the desk that had once been their father's—as though wiping it clean. 'Good, because she's not right for you.'

Loukas stared at Nikos, waiting for him to

smile, to admit that he was kidding. But instead Nikos held his gaze, his dark brown eyes steely.

'What the hell do you mean?'

Nikos didn't even flinch at his growl. 'Georgie is too flighty for you. I mean, she's a lot of fun, but she's not right for you.' He shrugged and said dismissively, 'She has nothing to offer you.'

Loukas shot out of his chair. 'I thought you were her friend. Do you even *know* her?'

He turned away from Nikos, almost sick with the amount of adrenaline coursing through his veins. He slammed the office door and twisted back to Nikos.

'Georgie's the most empathetic and kind and intelligent woman I have ever met!'

Despite himself, he couldn't keep his voice to a normal volume. Instead his words came out in an incredulous roar.

'And she has backbone—*real* backbone. She embraces life, she's independent, she challenges me. She's fun, and she gets this crazy family. She gets *me.*'

He knew he should stop. But he couldn't. The words were spilling out of him and his heart was close to exploding in his chest.

He marched over and stood glaring down at

Nikos, his heartbeat pounding in his ears, all rational thought long-departed. 'Georgie is everything I want.'

Nikos studied him carefully for a moment, his expression unimpressed. 'Have you told *her* any of this?'

Loukas stepped back and let out an angry breath. 'You've just played me, haven't you?'

Nikos gave a noncommittal shrug.

Loukas dropped to his chair. Lowering his head, he silently cursed Nikos as he swiped a hand over his brow. *Thee mou!* Had he really admitted what Georgie meant to him? To Nikos? To himself? These were feelings he didn't want to admit to. Because he hadn't a clue what to do with them.

He worked his jaw and jabbed a finger towards Nikos's computer screen. 'Show me the figures for the weekend.'

Nikos didn't move in his seat. 'Sounds to me like you're in love with her.'

'We're not having this conversation.'

Nikos scowled at him. 'This is just like when mum died.'

Once again Loukas shot out of his chair. 'What are you talking about?'

Nikos followed suit and stood, propping his

hands on his hips defiantly, anger firing in his eyes. 'It was impossible to talk to you. All you were interested in was the business.'

'It was you and Marios who refused to talk to *me*!'

Nikos stabbed a finger in his direction. 'Conversation is a two-way street, Loukas, and it's hard to open up to someone who gives nothing away, who refuses to share. You wanted us to talk to you about how we felt!' Nikos stopped and banged the tip of his brown brogue against the base of the desk. 'But this desk would have been more responsive, more empathetic.'

Really? Did they really have to talk about this? *Now?*

'I had to be strong for you.'

Nikos snarled at him. 'It felt like you didn't care!'

But then his shoulders slumped. He looked away. His fingers touched against the edge of his desk.

He drew in a deep breath before he looked up again, his eyes full of pain. 'Not once did you admit that you were hurting too, that you missed them.'

Loukas flinched at the bewilderment and anger and pain in Nikos's voice.

He twisted away to stare out of the window to one side of Nikos's office, his breath catching when he spotted Georgie, changed into jeans and a T-shirt, pedalling her bike away up the avenue. He wanted her to stay here on Talos. He wanted her to stay with *him*.

He turned back to Nikos. 'I saw how much you were all hurting and I didn't know how to deal with it. I was terrified of making things worse for you. I thought the thing you needed most was an adult in charge, someone who was in control, who was taking care of the business. I *did* care. I *did* hurt. I missed Mum and Dad… But what hurt most was seeing how devastated you were.'

Nikos dropped back to his seat. 'I wish you had told me how you were feeling back then—it would have made it a lot easier to share what I was going through.'

Nikos's brown eyes held his in the first true meaningful personal contact they had shared in years.

'Don't make the same mistake with Georgie. If you love her, tell her about your feelings for her. Don't shut her out.'

If only it was that straightforward. 'She's not into relationships.'

Nikos nodded. 'She's said that to me too. But, out in Reception, it looked to me as though you share something pretty special.'

Loukas ran a hand against the back of his neck, confusion weighing heavily in his chest. 'Maybe.'

When they'd made love, in those many small moments when she had smiled at him, he could have sworn that he saw love for him in her eyes.

He needed to find out what she felt for him. Unease twisted in his stomach. How would he cope if she said she felt nothing for him? How would he cope if she said she did? Was he really ready for the emotional rollercoaster that was love? Was he really ready to open himself up to all the vulnerability and insecurity that entailed?

'I've got to go. We'll talk through the figures tomorrow.'

Nikos plucked up a pencil from the desk and tapped it against the wood, his expression cool and defiant. 'No, I'll send you a management report at the end of the week, just like all of the other hotel managers in the group.'

'Fine.' Loukas knew he should just walk away, but the confusion and frustration within him was determined to let him have the last word. 'But the figures had better be good.'

Georgie ran her paintbrush along the wooden rail that sat on the garden wall and sang along with the song coming from the portable radio she had brought outside to distract her.

Her relationship with Loukas was nothing more than a fling. She needed to stop overthinking it and start putting things right by bringing it to a close. It *was* the right thing to do. Loukas deserved a partner—not for the crazy reason that he had to buy a hotel, but to marry someone who would support and care for him. Someone ambitious. Someone like Sofia Zisimos.

It wasn't fair either to raise Angeliki's hopes or expectations that there might be something more than a brief encounter between her and Loukas. And she needed to start protecting herself better.

'You're leaving brush marks.'

Georgie almost leapt out of her skin before twisting around and waving her paintbrush frantically at Loukas. 'Why did you creep up on me like that?'

Loukas raised his hands in the air as though it

was a gun she was pointing at him. 'I called out but you couldn't hear me with that song blaring out.'

He looked so gorgeous, standing there in faded denim jeans and a tight-fitting black T-shirt, the contours of his tanned biceps bulging as he held his arms up in surrender, a cute smile on his mouth.

She had to bring this to an end.

She gripped the paintbrush tighter. 'What are you doing here?'

That cute smile faded. 'We need to talk.'

Georgie turned away. Closed her eyes for a moment before she started to attack the railing with short furious brushstrokes. When he came and stood beside her she swallowed against the fear pounding through her veins.

He was clearly way ahead of her in ending their relationship. She wasn't sure if she could endure an *It was good while it lasted* conversation with him. She knew they needed to end their fling, but now that it was a reality it was a whole lot more painful than she'd expected.

She gave him a quick glance, tried to keep her voice nonchalant. 'Talk away.'

'I… I've grown fond of you, Georgie.'

She swung her head towards him. *Oh, for cry-*

ing out loud. She couldn't even stop trying to help him when he was trying to break things off with her. He was right. She really *did* have an unhealthy need to make life easier for other people.

She gave him a quick smile, wanting to get this over and done with. 'It's okay, Loukas, I know that it's over between you and me. Can I just ask that we leave it at that?' She turned back to her painting. 'Now, if you don't mind, I'm busy.'

Next thing she knew, Loukas was taking the paintbrush from her and looking at her curiously. 'I didn't come here to break it off. I came to ask if you'd consider moving in with me.'

She stared at him, slack-mouthed. His expression gave nothing away. Was he kidding her? Was this some sort of sick joke?

'Why?'

'I…' Loukas paused and looked down at the paintbrush he was now twisting in his palm. 'I think…' He looked up and for a moment she saw vulnerability in his gaze before he shrugged and said, with little enthusiasm, 'I guess we're good together.'

She took the paintbrush from him, plunged it into the paint pot. 'Next thing you'll be suggesting that we get married.'

'That's a possibility.'

She turned on him and jerked the loaded paint-brush towards him. 'This morning you didn't even want your family knowing about us and now you're talking about marriage. Are you *serious*?'

Her head was spinning. Why was he doing this to her?

Anger and confusion and pain merged and she pointed the paintbrush at him and demanded, 'All to buy a stupid hotel?'

His eyes narrowed. 'There's nothing stupid about me wanting to honour my father's promise to my mother. If he hadn't worked so hard for us all he'd still be here to buy it himself.'

'So let me get this right: you propose to honour the love between your mum and dad by having a loveless marriage yourself? Isn't that a little ironic? If not twisted?'

His hand shot forward and just in time he caught a drip of paint from her brush. Then those brown eyes of his met hers and for the longest time he stared at her.

Her heart beat crazily against her chest. This was the man she had made love with only this morning. Who had held her gently and whispered sweet words into her ear. And now she had no idea what was going on in his head.

She forced herself to hold his gaze, even though she felt sad and lonely and exposed at having been so intimate with this man and yet now feeling so detached from him.

Eventually he asked, 'Would it be a loveless marriage for you?'

She shook her head, trying to make sense of this conversation. 'Of course it would be a love-less marriage—a loving marriage can only exist when both people are in love.'

Loukas gritted his teeth, fighting the temptation to walk away. He was getting this all wrong.

His gut tightened. Talking about his emotions was alien to him. He had been brought up to be tough and resilient. And that toughness had swelled within him after his parents had died, shutting his emotions off.

His chest felt weighed down, as if a tangled mess of rope was pulling tighter and tighter... Could he really open himself up to Georgie? Risk the pain that might follow? But he couldn't let her go...not without at least trying to get her to stay.

He turned away and went to the outside tap to

wash his hands, buying time before he had to tell her exactly how he felt. The water was warm at first, but then it grew ice-cold.

A sickening feeling of fear and panic continued to twist through him. He had lost his mother and father…he didn't want to lose Georgie too.

The echo of his mum's last gasp had him flinching as he turned off the tap. How alone he'd felt as he had failed to control his own brutal sobs in that silent hospital room. And then there had been the journey home to his siblings. They had been sitting eating breakfast when he had reached the family villa, Angeliki and Marios fighting over who would eat the last of the sugar flakes. Nikos had silently watched him, and had refused to stay when he'd said they all needed to speak.

Loukas knew he had turned to work rather than having to face the feeling of failing his siblings every time he tried to get them to talk and they had looked at him blankly, angrily.

Maybe Nikos was right. If he had shown them by example that it was okay to express their emotions…if he had been honest about how much he missed their parents…then maybe they would have been more forthcoming in their feelings.

Georgie was attacking the railing with gusto, running her paintbrush in long strokes along the wood.

His mouth was dry, and despite the dropping temperature he felt unnaturally hot.

He went and stood beside her. 'I don't want you to leave Talos.'

She turned on him, those hazel eyes glittering with anger. 'I'm not taking part in a sham marriage.'

'I'm not asking you to. All I'm asking is that you stay here on Talos with me.'

She rubbed her hand against her forehead, leaving a trail of blue paint behind. 'Why?'

Her tone was incredulous. Was she really that blind to his feelings for her? Had he got it so wrong in reading her feelings for him?

He should turn away now. This was never going to work. Georgie had always said she was a nomad, and not interested in relationships.

But what if there was a chance that she'd change her mind once she knew how he felt? Could he spend the rest of his life wondering what would have happened if he had had the courage to tell her the truth of his feelings for her?

He inhaled a deep breath. 'Don't you see it, Georgie?'

'See what?'

'I've fallen in love with you.'

She lifted her hand and held it over her mouth, her long fingers touching against her lips, horror etched in her eyes.

He felt as though he had been cut in half by a high-velocity weapon.

He gritted his teeth against the acute pain lacerating his heart and from somewhere deep inside him found a nonchalant voice. 'You're supposed to say something back to me now.'

She blinked. Made several attempts to talk before she finally managed to. 'This isn't what we agreed to.'

He had fallen in *love* with her. Had he *really* said those words to her? Was he telling the truth? Or was this just a ploy to get her to agree to marry him?

This wasn't what she wanted.

She drew back. Winced at the bewilderment in Loukas's expression that was fast turning to anger.

He crossed his arms. 'You don't believe me, do you?'

She tried to talk but no words came. She shrugged. Then shook her head. Not even sure herself what she was silently trying to say to him.

He couldn't love her. And even if he thought he did now, some day he would realise that he didn't. And then he'd walk away from her.

She gestured towards the house. 'I need to get a jumper.'

She ran towards the house and into her bedroom. There, she stared blindly into her wardrobe, overwhelmed and confused.

Eventually she remembered why she was standing there and grabbed the first jumper she could find.

Outside she tried to pass Loukas, needing the distraction of painting—anything to avoid looking him squarely in the eye—but he reached out and stopped her, his expression a mixture of bewilderment and hurt.

'Have you anything to say to me?'

I don't know! I just... I just... I'm scared, Loukas. And confused. And overwhelmed. I want you to be able to see the fear inside me and hold me and tell me everything will be okay. But who am I to expect that from you? And look what I've done to you...look at the pain and anger in your eyes. You don't deserve this.

She closed her eyes for a moment before saying, 'I've decided to stay here tonight.'

He drew back. His eyes were shuttered. 'By yourself?' His tone was cold and detached.

Was she doing the right thing? Was she really prepared to let this man go? She felt numb, unable to think.

She wavered, winced at the icy fury forming in his eyes, then said, 'Yes, by myself.'

He inhaled a long slow breath. 'Will you be back at work tomorrow?'

Why had she slept with him? Everything had changed after that. The intensity of the connection between them, her feelings for him, had all muddled up ever since. She had blown it. Now they could never even be friends. It was *she* who knew she could never be in a relationship...she shouldn't have done this to him.

In a low voice she eventually answered, 'Maybe it's for the best if I don't.'

He stared at her as though he hated her. 'That's your decision to make.'

She blinked. 'No…no, I won't be at work to-morrow.'

He nodded and walked away.

As he opened the garden door she called out, 'I'm not what you need, Loukas, don't you see that?'

He stopped and gave a bitter laugh. 'You seem determined to make me believe that, whether I want to or not.'

With that he walked out into the fading light of the day.

CHAPTER TEN

GEORGIE RAPPED HER glass against those of the four men standing out on her terrace. In unison they all said, *'Yamas!'*

Georgie took a deep gulp of ouzo. The fiery liquid exploded in her mouth, the anise flavour burning a trail down her throat.

She lifted the glass again and took another gulp, liking how much it hurt.

Sokratis, her building contractor, had emptied his glass in one go. 'Will you be okay here on your own, Georgie, now that we're finished?'

Why did every person on the island ask her that question?

'I'm looking forward to the peace!'

You're such a liar, Georgie.

Well, what do you expect me to say? The truth? Something along the lines of, Well, actually, Sokratis, I'm really going to miss the noise and confusion of you four arriving every morning.

Now I'll have no distraction from my thoughts and my guilt.

'And Loukas?'

Her attention turned to Theofanis, the carpenter in the group. His quiet, gentle nature and mastery with wood so at odds with his giant frame and shovel-like hands.

She smiled and tried not to look bothered by his question, but it hurt just to hear Loukas's name said out loud. 'What about him?'

'You're together, no? I saw you together in the square at the Easter Midnight service.'

She took another swig of her ouzo. The fiery liquid did nothing to numb the ache in her throat. 'No.'

Theofanis shook his head and looked at her sadly. 'He's a good man.'

'I know.'

'He's brought a lot of employment and prosperity to the island,' said Giourkas, another member of the building team, with a hint of accusation.

All four men considered her coolly.

Oh, great. Now she'd upset the locals. No doubt they wouldn't take kindly to her breaking up with their local hero.

She stared down at the dusty boots of the four men.

'He's even fought for regional funding. It was Loukas who secured the subsidy for the new marina in Talos Town,' Sokratis said.

All four men nodded in silence, clearly privately reflecting on the wonder that was Loukas Christou.

Georgie clutched her glass tighter. This was the man who had said he loved her.

'He looked after my cousin Kyriakos when he was ill. He works as a gardener at the hotel. He kept his job open and paid him all the time he was undergoing treatment. Well over a year. He even gave his family the use of his own private boat to take them to Kosta when he needed treatment,' Theofanis added.

Álexandros, Sokratis's son, shook his head in amazement. 'Wow, that's a powerful boat.'

Georgie let out a sigh. 'Okay, I get it. The man's a saint.'

Theofanis lifted an eyebrow. 'Well, I wouldn't go that far. He can be stubborn, and more headstrong than a herd of goats.'

'And competitive,' Alexandros said with relish. 'We were at school together. He had to win everything. One year he even entered and won the embroidery competition.'

Giourkas lifted the blue and white baseball cap he always wore and scratched his thatch of thick black hair. 'Now, that's just *strange*.'

'His father drove him hard,' Sokratis said, shaking his head disapprovingly. 'When the hotel first opened I was the maintenance manager. Loukas, even as a very young boy, used to be up and working in the hotel before sunrise. Even on the soccer pitch he pushed him hard. *Thee mou*, that man could yell. He would leave Loukas to walk home alone when his team lost…sometimes even when they won and Loukas hadn't scored.'

Alexandros grimaced and ran a hand along his bristled jawline. 'He didn't score full marks in an exam at school once. We all thought he was joking when he asked the teacher to check his paper again. Maybe he was nervous about going home?'

All four men looked at each other uncomfortably, and then down at their now empty glasses. Georgie's glass was still half full, but even looking at the ouzo made her feel ill. Loukas had told her of his relationship with his dad, but hearing about it from others made it all the more real. No wonder he pushed himself so hard.

She was startled when Sokratis cleared his throat noisily and said, 'It's time we headed for home.'

Georgie followed the men out through her garden door. Sokratis untied his dapple-grey horse from where it had been sheltering under a tree and placed a harness on its broad back before attaching it to his cart. The others had retrieved their bikes and she waved goodbye to them.

Sokratis, now seated on the wooden bench at the front of his cart, drew level with her and regarded her solemnly from beneath his bushy eyebrows. 'It's a gift in life to be able to recognise when you're not happy and to do something about it. Be brave, Georgie.'

Georgie stared after Sokratis as his cart moved up the track, totally taken aback. She had thought she *was* coping. For the past four days she had risen before dawn and worked until late into the night. Refusing to think. Determined to get the villa ready for her first guests. She was proud of what she had achieved. Her dad would be too. The house and gardens had been transformed into a cosy and welcoming guesthouse.

She was proud...but Sokratis was right. She wasn't happy. The truth of the matter was that she didn't even know if she could bear to stay here on Talos for the summer months.

Only days ago she had harboured the fantasy that she and Loukas would be able to remain friends whatever happened between them. But that had been before they had made love...before they'd clung to one another and stared into one another's eyes.

She had been wrong to allow what they had between them become so serious.

Back inside the house, she dropped down onto the new sofa Sokratis had transported to the house earlier that day and stared at her phone, sitting on the coffee table. All day she had refused to look, but now with a sigh she grabbed the phone and scanned her social media newsfeeds.

She paused at the selfie Angeliki had taken in a limo on her way to the movie awards last night, and laughed into the empty space of her sitting room at Angeliki's bright-eyed, thumbs-up picture.

Angeliki had visited on Wednesday, bluntly telling her she wanted to know what was going on between her and Loukas. Georgie had tried not to wince when Angeliki had asked if what Loukas had said was true—that it was all over between them.

When Georgie had said it was, Angeliki had at first stormed around the house, proclaiming that they were both idiotic, but when she'd calmed Georgie had seen just how disappointed she really was. Georgie had spent the afternoon with her, slowly and gently reassuring her that they would remain friends despite everything.

She scanned some more posts, and closed her eyes for a moment when she came upon a picture of Loukas, standing with his three siblings on the red carpet inside the hotel's reception area. The three brothers were all wearing tuxedos, Loukas in the middle, his arms around Nikos's and Marios's shoulders. Angeliki was in front of him, leaning back against him, her beaded full-skirted white ball gown stunning against her dark skin and hair.

She stared at the image of Loukas on her phone, at the strength of his expression, the cool pride in his eyes, her heart aching for him. And slowly it finally dawned on her that this was it. It really was all over between her and Loukas. He was moving on with his life. And it was time that she did too.

It was time she left this island.

* * *

Loukas's head felt as if it was about to explode. He had the headache to end all headaches, and now he had Nikos, Marios and Angeliki going off-message again, thinking with their hearts and not their brains.

He leant back in his boardroom chair and said, with as much civility he could muster, 'Run that by me again. I think I must have misheard you.'

Angeliki cast a nervous glance at Nikos. Marios rolled his eyes.

Nikos leant towards him and flashed him one of his killer smiles. 'You heard right. We're not going to sign off on the purchase of the Amalfi hotel until you get back with Georgie.'

They *had* to be kidding him.

'We've spent a fortune setting up this deal—we have competitors keen to snatch it away. Are you all out of your minds?'

He leapt up and paced the boardroom floor. The purchase of the Convento San Francesco was already in tatters, thanks to his ill-judgement and the fact that, despite Zeta finding some promising candidates, he just couldn't bring himself to go on a date at the moment. There was no hope

260 TEMPTED BY HER GREEK TYCOON

of him finding a wife anytime soon, but this deal had to go through.

'This isn't how you run a business.'

Angeliki winced, but she had a determined glint in her eye that frankly scared him.

'We're not asking you to negotiate a UN peace agreement, Loukas, simply to sort things out between you and Georgie.'

'There's nothing to sort out.'

Nikos tapped a pen against the glass top of the boardroom table. 'I have no idea what she sees in you, as you're so bloody-minded and cranky, but she *liked* you, Loukas. She really liked you.'

Nikos threw his pen on to the table and regarded him with a mixture of pity and disappointment. 'I thought you were going to sort things out with her... I do hope you realise what a mistake you're making—she's the best thing to ever have happened to you.'

Right then Loukas's head exploded. 'Do you think I don't *know* that? Do you think I don't *know* that she's the most beautiful, annoying, fun, uplifting, wise person I have ever met? The one person I can talk to.'

He stopped shouting. Looked at the shocked expressions of the others. Dropped to his seat and looked at his siblings helplessly. For the first time ever he was reaching out to them emotionally… no longer caring about looking weak in front of them, no longer caring that there was no dignity in what he was about to admit.

'I've told her that I love her… It was Georgie who ended the relationship, not me.'

All three stared at him, and the only sound in the room came from the air conditioning unit.

Angeliki was the first to speak. 'I'm sorry, Loukas.'

Then, taking the sale contract for the hotel, she signed it.

Marios silently reached for it and signed it too. When he was done he nodded towards Loukas. It was a nod full of allegiance.

Nikos then signed the document and walked towards Loukas.

Handing him the contract, he placed a hand on Loukas's shoulder. 'Welcome to the heartbreak club, brother.'

A week later Georgie found a quiet spot on the deck of the ferry that would take her to Athens. From there she would catch a flight to Stockholm.

The past week had been a blur of organisation—

arranging for Ourania Riga, the head chef at the Koozina Restaurant, to rent her house from her, organising her own accommodation in Stockholm.

Thankfully she had been able to transfer all her booked guests to another guesthouse on the island, and Marios had agreed to add the sea-swimming tours to his business.

It hadn't been easy to persuade him. And she had received an equally frosty reception from Nikos and Angeliki when she had visited them at their apartment to say goodbye.

Beyond the white railings of the ferry Talos Town glistened in the early-morning sun. She ran both hands tiredly over her face.

Leaving was different than she had anticipated. Where was the excitement for her new adventure? Why did she feel so lonely?

Sitting on the hard plastic chair on the ferry, her suitcases crowded at her feet, she felt the reality of her situation, the reality of what she was about to do, hit her for the first time.

It was as though she had numbly spent the past week in a cloud of self-delusion. Believing foolishly that she could just move on—yes, she'd miss Talos and the Christou family...she'd miss

Loukas, but she'd done this time and time again. Moved on. Created a new life for herself.

Believing this was no different.

But it *was* different.

Talos, this island of fragrances and emerald seas was different from anywhere she had been before.

The friends she had made here were different too. Vasilis had almost cried when she'd called to say goodbye to him last night. Nikos, Marios and Angeliki, despite their coolness, had all tried to persuade her to stay. When she had said no they had hugged her generously and wished her well.

And then there was Loukas.

Has he really meant it when he'd said he loved her? Her mother had been supposed to love her, yet she'd left. How could she believe that *he* loved her?

She stood and walked to the railing. Stared up towards the church where they had watched the Easter fireworks together with his arms wrapped tightly around her.

When they had first met he had been so serious and closed. But as they had grown closer she had seen the integrity, the kindness, the honour inside him.

Her mind looped back to her conversation with

Sokratis and his team. Their description of his relationship with his dad. No wonder he was so closed and wary. No wonder he drove himself so hard.

Her eyes widened.

How much must it have taken for him to open up to me?

And then it hit her. Loukas wouldn't admit to love easily. He wouldn't say those words unless he meant them. She had been totally blind. She had been so taken up by the fears inside herself that she had ignored every single fact she knew about the man who'd told her that he loved her. His loyalty and integrity, his honour, the way he had unselfishly spent the past eight years focused only on protecting his family. How tenderly he had made love to her. The love that had shone in his eyes when they had teased one another.

The ferry's horn hooted—the traditional call to any straggling passengers up in Talos Town that it was going to depart in five minutes.

She was two floors up.

She had to make a decision.

But how could she make this right?

Where would she even start?

She closed her eyes for a moment, felt all the

loneliness and pain inside her sharpening in the momentary darkness.

She had to talk to him.

This unsettled feeling, the way she ached to be with him again, was a thousand times worse than any of her fears.

She grabbed her suitcases and pushed her way down the two flights of stairs as the cases careened off the railings and smacked into the back of her legs.

She made it to the gangway just before they pulled it away.

On the quayside she loaded her luggage onto a carriage and asked the driver to take it to her friend Stefania's jewellery gallery. She sent Stefania a quick text, asking if she'd store it in her office for a few hours.

And then she walked towards The Korinna, her heart performing somersaults and her legs so weak as she walked up the pedestrian alleyway that one of the elderly residents passed her by on the steep climb upwards with a cheery *'Kaliméra!'*.

What if Loukas wanted nothing to do with her now? What if she had blown it with him in her disbelief when he had told her that he loved her?

She walked down the hotel avenue, through the orchard, and at the villa's garden door paused, her entire body shaking. Would he even be at home?

He was. In fact he was standing at the edge of the terrace, close to the rocky outcrop, staring at the ferry as it left the harbour.

He was dressed in a charcoal suit, his broad shoulders taut, his stance alert and controlled. A modern-day Greek warrior.

He must have sensed her, because he slowly turned around, brief surprise flashing in his eyes before he crossed his arms on that powerful chest she had so many times laid her head upon and eyed her coolly.

She gave an automatic nervous smile.

His grimace tightened.

'I was supposed to leave for Athens today,' she said.

'So I heard.'

'On the ferry this morning I realised that I couldn't leave.'

His only response was an impatient resettling of his arms on his chest.

She dragged in a long, slow breath. Though it terrified her, she knew she had to open herself up to him, tell him everything that was inside her. It was time she showed him that she loved him.

She moved towards him, her breath hitching when she was within arm's reach of him and saw the guarded expression in his eyes.

She dipped her head, suddenly realising, now that she was standing so close to him, just how much she had missed him physically over the past two weeks.

Her hands itched with the need to touch him. She wanted to place her lips against his skin. His mouth. To touch the silky softness of his hair, the hard lines of his shoulders. To have him tuck her into his side the way he liked to do, so that her belly was pressed against his hip. Most of all she wanted him to look at her with the same love and tenderness, fondness and wonder with which he had gazed at her every time they had made love.

She lifted her head, her heart in her throat, and said, 'I'm sorry for the way I reacted…on the day you told me you loved me.'

He looked beyond her, towards the house. 'I thought we had something.'

She winced at the coldness in his voice. 'We did. We still can…'

He gave her a sceptical look.

She rubbed her hands on the denim of her jeans, feeling hot and clammy. 'I should have seen how much courage it had taken for you to tell me you loved me. I should have believed you. Instead I pushed you away.'

He raised an eyebrow at this, as if to say, *Tell me something I don't know.*

She bit the inside of her lip, trying to dredge up the courage to tell him everything he needed to know, all the while fighting the deep fear inside her that she would be exposing herself to future pain.

She inhaled a quick breath and started to talk before that fear took control. 'Every relationship I've been in, whether romantic or a friendship, I've run away, afraid of growing too close, afraid of being hurt. I'm tired of running, but I find it hard to believe that you love me… What can I give you? I'm not the tough career wife you want. And you said yourself that you don't have time in your life for love. I panic that you'll leave me. I panic so much that I just want to run away be-fore I get hurt…*again.*'

She wrapped her hands around her waist, over

the soft jersey fabric of her sweater, waited for him to speak.

He shook his head, annoyed. 'But *why* do you think I'd leave you? That I would lie about something as important as admitting that I love you? Do you know me at *all*, Georgie?'

'I do… I know how strong and loyal and protective you are. But it's not about you—it's me that's messed up. My mum walking out…seeing my dad so unhappy…the nature of my childhood… it's all messed me up. Almost twenty years after my mum left I'm still gutted…and I don't know how I would ever cope if you did the same.'

He dropped his arms and slowly ran a hand along his jaw, his expression confused. He moved away, turned and stared out to sea.

When he turned back it was with that sceptical expression again. 'Why didn't you leave for Athens today? Why are you here, Georgie? Is this all about your compulsion to make other people happy? Well, I don't need your pity.'

'No! Of course not.' She stopped and swallowed, knowing she was about to say the most important words she would ever say to another person and she had no idea how he would react. 'I'm here because I want to tell you that I love you.'

She was standing staring at him, with her eyes full of fear, and every instinct in him wanted to go to Georgie and hold her. To believe her words...believe that she loved him.

They were words that should change everything. But he had spent his childhood looking for his father's love and approval, constantly afraid that he would fail him, his family, his responsibilities. He needed more from Georgie. He *had* to be sure of her love. He needed her to trust him. To value him. He needed to feel safe in this relationship.

He arched his neck and fixed her with a steady gaze. 'Why do you love me?'

Georgie eyed him nervously, looking more like a terrified job applicant at an interview than a woman explaining why she was in love with a man.

She wrung her hands and then, almost in a whisper, her voice trembling, said, 'I love how you protect your family, your staff, the community.' She paused and worried at her lip. 'I love how much you care for every guest who comes to your hotel. I love your loyalty and kindness to others.'

Her jaw worked for a moment. Were those tears shining in her eyes?

She cleared her throat. 'When we're together everything feels right. With you I finally feel like I've found the place where I belong in my life.'

'How can I be sure that you won't run away in the future?'

She looked at him helplessly. 'I'll… I'll give you my word…'

She said those words in such a low voice that it touched something in him. Without thinking he heard himself speak, his voice echoing with the torture and bitterness and pain that had been living inside him since the day he had told Georgie he loved her.

'I didn't want to fall in love with you. Especially knowing about your restlessness, how you felt about relationships. But I *did* fall in love with you. And I'm just as scared as you are.'

He paused, realised he was trembling.

'I need to know that you trust me not to abandon you…but equally I need to know that you won't one day just leave, run away again.'

She nodded, but she was still looking as lost and confused as he was feeling. She dropped her head, as though deep in thought, and then back up and spoke to tentatively. 'I know how important it is for you to buy that hotel in Florence—'

He interrupted her. 'Not as important as you are.'

She blinked at that, tears flooding her eyes for a moment. 'Perhaps we need to give each other time—time to show one another that we won't do any of those things. I'm tired of running, Loukas. Most of all I'm tired of running away from my fears. I need and I love this island, and your crazy family, but most all I need and love *you*. In the future I will still want to travel—but with you at my side, knowing that we will be returning to Talos. For the next year I want to stay here on Talos, to put down roots. I want to show you that I can change, that I won't leave. I know that you'll have to go away for work, and although this might sound a little crazy even having you leave the island for work will freak me out a little bit… I'll worry you won't come back, but I want you to leave so that I can prove to you that I know deep down that you'll never abandon me.'

Her voice had been hoarse and thick with emotion, her eyes scared and yet brave, and her body was shaking. The woman he loved stood there, reaching out to him. Prepared to show him how much she trusted, needed, loved him.

He shrugged off his suit jacket and held it out for her to put on over her light weight sweater. She tried to object, but then she paused, gave him a small smile and placed her arms into the sleeves.

It was time he told her properly why he loved her—not in the fearful and cautious way he had tried to tell her the first time around.

Taking her hand in his, he led her down to the small sandy cove below the villa. There he sat directly opposite her, his heart knocking loudly, fear stirring in his stomach that he wouldn't find the right words.

'You're right when you say that you're not the tough career wife I thought I wanted. But you're so much more than I ever dreamed I would find.'

Georgie smiled at him shyly. His heart swelled with love for her.

'You bring an optimism, a lightness into my life that has been missing for way too long. You bring an empathy and understanding of others that I miss because I can be so wrapped up in business and the bottom line, and the echoes of my dad's voice telling me that I must never fail.'

They were both sitting on the sand with their

knees bent, her left leg captured between his. A light breeze was flickering against the tendrils of hair that had escaped from her ponytail.

He reached out and tucked them behind her ear before continuing, 'You've given me back my family…you've opened up a whole new world of understanding for me.'

He reached down and touched the delicate skin covering her shinbone beneath her jeans. So much of her was delicate—the fine bones in her face, the shape of her ears, the slenderness of her neck—but inside she was one of the bravest, most astute people he had ever met.

'When I told you that I loved you and you didn't say anything back I panicked. I felt so exposed. I had no idea how you felt about me… I just knew that you were pushing me away and didn't need me.'

Georgie winced and said gently, 'Sorry…'

He shook his head. 'I was so wrapped up in my own feelings of hurt and fear that I couldn't see that you were panicking because I was moving too quickly. How many times had you told me that you weren't into relationships? Because of your mum leaving…all of the friends you've lost.'

She gave a half-smile. 'Yes, but I should have said something about how much I love you.'

He nodded. 'Perhaps. But you were scared. I should have given you time, let you build your trust in me, proved to you that our relationship could work—proved to you just how much I adore you and need you in my life.'

'But what if I do the same again in the future? Hurt you? Panic for some reason and try to push you away?'

'We'll work through it. One step at a time. No rushing. You're right—we do need to give this time. Let's just date for a while, see where that takes us. I want us to have fun and get to know one another.'

She gave him another shy smile. 'I feel like I know you so well already.'

He ran his fingers further up her calf. 'There's still so much for you to find out.'

She giggled and tried to pull away. 'Don't tell me that you have super-powers?'

'No, but I do make the best home-made ice cream ever. And I've developed an obsession with midnight swimming.'

That mischievous sunshine smile he loved so

much was back on her lips. 'I don't suppose you'd like to come for a swim now?'

He raised an eyebrow. And then, swinging forward, grabbed her hands and fell backwards onto the sand so she landed on top of him. 'Hi, Georgie Jones.'

'Hi, Loukas Christou.'

'Have I told you that I love you?'

'Yes, you've told me…'

Those cherub's lips of hers moved towards his and her eyes darkened.

Her voice came out in a breathy whisper. 'But I think you should show me now…'

EPILOGUE

A YEAR LATER the Easter Sunday lunch table had expanded considerably.

Vasilis had joined them again, but this year he was accompanied by his son Demis and Demis's girlfriend Maja, who were visiting Talos for the Pascha celebrations.

Marios was busy extolling the virtues of Talos to Swedish-born Maja, keen to persuade her and Demis to return to live on the island...especially as Maja happened to be a qualified diving instructor, and he needed more instructors for his ever-expanding diving school.

Angeliki had also returned home from the Christou Plaka hotel in Athens for the weekend, her eyes glowing with excitement and pride at settling so easily into her new role and life as Deputy Manager in the hotel. And Angeliki had not come home alone. A medical student from the University of Athens had accompanied her, and the poor guy was doing his best not to be cowed by Angeliki's three burly older brothers, who were interrogating him at every available opportunity.

Also at the table this year were Mr and Mrs Dias, back on Talos to celebrate their golden wedding anniversary.

Vasilis was busy entertaining the guests at the table by reading everyone's coffee grounds.

There was a moment's consternation when Vasilis announced to Nikos that he saw a baby in his imminent future. Nikos paled, while Loukas looked at him decidedly unimpressed. Nikos raised his hands in self-defence and swore vehemently that he wasn't dating *anyone* at the moment. And then he laughed heartily when Vasilis announced that he was mistaken and that it was *Loukas's* coffee grounds he had read.

At that point Loukas stared in Georgie's direction, his look of thrilled amazement making her blush.

Loukas stood up and dragged Nikos inside, leaving her with the task of having to convince the rest of the guests that they really didn't have any news to share with them.

The house band broke into a rendition of 'Why Do Fools Fall in Love?' as Loukas and Nikos appeared back on the terrace, carrying an enormous cake covered in rich golden buttercream and gold leaf.

Mrs Dias gave a little cry of happiness and wagged her finger at Georgie, now understanding why Georgie had asked yesterday if there was any song that reminded her of their wedding day. Applause and cheers rang out across the terrace as Loukas and Nikos laid the cake before Mr and Mrs Dias. Both had tears in their eyes when they stood and cut into the cake that would be shared amongst all the guests as part of the dessert buffet the hotel staff were assembling now the main courses had been cleared away.

As the rest of the guests' attention returned to their own tables and the band began to play another song, Mr Dias asked Georgie to translate something he wanted to say.

Georgie hushed everyone at the table and then, with a lump in her throat, moved her gaze over Loukas and his siblings.

'Mr Dias asked me to tell you that he's certain that your mother and father would be very proud of what you have achieved in the business but in particular that you have remained so united.'

All four looked at Mr Dias with grateful smiles.

But then Nikos had to go and ruin it all when he muttered, 'He wouldn't say that if he'd witnessed our last board meeting.'

'For the last time, Nikos, expanding into the Asian market isn't viable right now.' Loukas's gaze shot over to Marios, who was about to interrupt. 'And don't even *start* talking about introducing water zorbing. It doesn't fit with our five-star status.'

Angeliki leapt forward and gave Loukas a *Got you!* look. 'I don't know about that—look how wrong you were about the water trampolines. The guests love them.' Angeliki paused and raised an eyebrow. 'And I'm sure I saw you and Georgie out on one late last night… Don't you dare deny it, Loukas—look at how much Georgie is blushing.'

Loukas shot out of his chair. 'I think it's time for Tsougrisma.'

Despite her embarrassment Georgie felt something crack in her heart at the sight of her cool-headed boyfriend so flustered and—more than that—the good-humoured affection shining in his siblings' eyes as they watched him hand out a red egg to everyone at the table.

The final game ended up being between a much-excited Maja and Loukas. Once again the entire table groaned when Loukas inevitably won.

But of course, with the chivalry and kindness Georgie had witnessed from him time and time again over the past year, Loukas insisted that Maja keep his egg.

Georgie watched Maja hug him in thanks, and she loved him even more.

At Angeliki's insistence everyone stood and made their way to the dance floor, but Loukas drew Georgie back so that they were standing alone under the terrace canopy.

Would she ever tire of staring into those soft brown eyes? Of touching her hand against the hard ridge of his jawline? Would she ever be able to resist wrapping her arms around his narrow waist and resting her head against his rock-hard chest, hearing his solid heartbeat?

She smiled up at him. But then her smile faded. Why was he so nervous? He wasn't even able to look her directly in the eye.

What was wrong?

Loukas worked his jaw. Gazed at her with a small uncertain smile. And then he reached into the pocket of his suit jacket. Holding out his palm to her, he said in a low voice, 'This is for you.'

In the middle of his palm lay a delicate red Fabergé-style egg, crafted with bands of gold and inset diamonds.

Her heart leapt into her throat. She lifted the egg. It was heavier than she'd expected, and so beautiful that tears popped into her eyes.

She blinked for a few moments, cleared her throat. 'Are you sure...? It looks very expensive.'

With a laugh, Loukas asked, 'Aren't you going to open it?'

It opened?

Georgie turned the egg and saw a tiny clasp in the middle that she hadn't spotted before. Undoing the clasp, she opened up the egg.

She gasped and shut the lid.

Her gaze shot to his.

His earlier nervousness was still there, but there was also determination.

Reaching for her hand, he said, 'Let's go for a walk.'

He led her to the orchard and under a lemon blossom tree ran his fingertips against her cheek and down the length of her arm, his intense, loving, tender gaze never wavering from hers.

'A year ago I was crashing all over the place— messing up my relationship with my family, consumed with guilt and in constant fear of failing. And then you cycled into my life—this crazy mermaid who made me realise that I needed to let that fear go in order to really start living. You *complete* me. With you I have grown stronger, more secure in myself. I just hope that I have supported you in a similar way.'

She nodded and nodded and nodded, her mouth hurting because she was smiling so much.

'Of course you do. Your support and strength and your belief in me has settled me. I no longer feel so adrift and restless. I love it here on Talos—spending the summer months at my house, the winter months here in your villa. And I love our neighbours...' She paused and gave him a cheeky look. 'I'm still working on loving their goats, but I'm getting there.'

Her insides went all mushy at the sound of his laughter. She gently ran her thumb against the egg still in her palm. 'I love your family. For the first time since I was a little girl I truly feel as though I have found home...a place where I belong. Thank you for everything you have given me... I love you more and more with each passing day.'

Taking the egg from her, Loukas went down before her on one knee and opened the egg, presented it to her. The solitaire diamond on a platinum band shone brilliantly in the dappled shade.

Fresh tears rushed to her eyes.

'Are you ready for the next step in our journey together?'

She nodded, her heart so full of love and wonder that she struggled to speak. But eventually she managed to say, 'Yes, I am.'

'Georgie Jones, will you marry me?'

She laughed. And then she sobbed. And then she flapped her hands wildly. 'Of *course* I'll marry you.'

And even though she must look a mess, with red-rimmed eyes, Loukas stood and stared at her as though she was the most incredible thing he had ever seen. And then he kissed her. A kiss full of tenderness and promises.

When he pulled away his eyes sparkled with happiness. 'Big wedding or small wedding?'

Georgie laughed. 'Do we have a choice?'

He chuckled. 'Not really. The islanders would probably riot if we kept it small.'

She touched her hand to the high planes of his cheekbone, down over the jawline that was already showing signs of evening shadow. 'Good, because I want a big, glorious, noisy Greek wed-

ding so I can spend the entire day telling everyone just how much I love you.'

He drew her hand from his jawline and, taking
the ring from the white silk pillow it was sitting
on, placed it on her finger.

'No more running?'

She laughed. Popped a kiss on his lips. And then
she smiled and smiled and smiled, ready to burst
with happiness.

'Not when I've found where I belong.'

* * * * *

LET'S TALK

Romance

For exclusive extracts, competitions and special offers, find us online:

f facebook.com/millsandboon

⬜ @millsandboonuk

🐦 @millsandboon

Or get in touch on 0844 844 1351*

For all the latest titles coming soon, visit millsandboon.co.uk/nextmonth